M000197930

ISBN Paperback: 9781735771564

Cover Design: Mayflower Studio

Editing: Bookish Dreams Editing

Proofreading: Bookish Dreams Editing and Proof Before You Publish.

❀ Created with Vellum

CONTENTS

FOREWORD

AUTHOR'S NOTE

This book is a Reverse Harem romance. The heroine does not have to choose between male interests. This book has a FMMMMM relationship. Recommended for 18+ due to mature content.

DEDICATION

Mom — you're the best! Thanks for being my biggest cheerleader and for letting me draft you into being a beta reader. Love you!

1

ARDEN

The dark grey warehouse looms silently before me. *Is this the right place?* I glance down at the map on my phone and back up to the street sign. *Yes, this is it.* My eyes scan the building for an entrance, but I don't find one. Puzzled, I walk across the street to get a better view.

The size of a city block, the structure looks even more imposing from this perspective. I crane my neck, searching for an entrance, but dark grey, painted bricks stretch the entire block without relief. No doors or windows. I sit on the curb for a second to think.

Arrgh. I barely refrain from smacking my forehead.

My magic traces lightly over the building, encountering an obsidian wall, not a part of the building, but a wall of wards so powerful and ancient, it makes my magic feel insignificant in comparison. Shivering, I brush the wards lightly with my magic and convey my desire to enter.

A script boldly appears on the side of the building. "The Abbey."

This is definitely the right place.

In the center of the building, two massive black doors stand tall with a glowing mark on each of them—an infinity within a circle. The ancient symbol means sanctuary for all supernaturals, a place where beings of all races can come together, without fear of death or reprisal from their individual rulers.

Several sanctuaries exist throughout the world. This particular haven is called The Abbey in reference to the ancient church which stood in its place previously. Ley lines, the conveyors of magic, cross at multiple points beneath the building. The combination of natural power and sacred ground is the perfect foundation for a sanctuary, using natural resources instead of personal magic to maintain the wards.

Sanctuaries are owned and managed by cadres, groups of supernaturals from distinct races, typically of like power, who form a sacred bond. Their bond and combined magic create an astronomical force of power capable of enforcing the rules of sanctuary. In addition, while they often serve the supernatural council, the cadres exist as a non-partisan body because only their bond is held in the highest regard, nothing else. This makes them the perfect sanctuary guardians.

This sanctuary in particular is owned by the Imperium Cadre, five of the most powerful supernaturals in existence. This group of warriors includes an Elven prince, a Fae lord, a warlock, the First Vampire, and the King of Dragons. Individually, their power rivals few in our world, but together, they're a powerhouse.

And I'm going in there to ask them for a favor, possibly more than one, all so I can find the destiny that's ruled my isolated life. I'm a witch with a lot of questions, few answers, and a need for allies.

I stand, brush off my clothes, and take a deep breath. *The first step is always the hardest, right?* Nodding to myself, I find my center, wrap my shield around me like a cloak, and head across the street.

My fingertips graze the sanctuary symbol for luck. With a slight push, I open one of the black doors. Although massive, they open easily and smoothly. I step through the wards into a cool, dark interior, where magic pulses in the walls and permeates the very air I'm breathing—a mixture of spells and wards designed to keep The Abbey, and its inhabitants, safe. It's so thick, I can taste it.

When my eyes focus, I realize it's a club. A multitude of black tables and chairs surround a massive dance floor, with a DJ booth sitting on a raised platform in the back. Not that I've been in many clubs, but Callyx used to take me to a similar club in the Underworld.

A golden glint catches my eye, so I walk over and glance down at the sparkling dance floor. Gold glitter is embedded into the smooth black surface, and it's sort of glowing, too.

Is it a spotlight? Looking up, I don't see one, but I spot several stories above this one, each neatly stacked on top of the other, with the dance floor as the central focus. Given the inky darkness, I can't quite see the number of floors or their purpose. What's interesting is the building appears to be two stories tall from the outside. I raise my eyebrows at the use of power required to either conceal the true height of the building or to create a pocket dimension within the sanctuary itself.

As I walk to the left, a gleaming ebony bar rises from the darkness, and a pair of golden cat eyes stare at me from behind it. Walking slowly but confidently towards the bar, I watch the eyes narrow in appraisal and hear the sound of someone sniffing the air.

Once I'm closer, the golden eyes meld into the face of a beautiful woman who's standing behind the bar with a clipboard. She's tall, athletic looking, and her long hair, a combination of blondes and browns, flows wildly around her firm jaw and high cheekbones.

"Hello, witch. We're currently closed, and we're not hiring. You can come back around eight p.m. when we open," her smooth voice purrs.

Meeting her golden eyes, I tell her, "I'm here to see Lord Theron. Is he available?"

"He's not available. I can take a message, if you like?" Her voice is terse as she looks at me with suspicion.

A whisper of air moves behind me, and goosebumps rise on my arm. Someone else is definitely here, but nobody comes into the light. "Yes, that would be wonderful, thank you," I reply as I hand her a golden card with the Fae royal seal embossed on it. Only the recipient of the intended message will see the actual number.

She glances at the card, noting the royal seal, and then shifts her gaze back up at me. Her eyes wide, she asks, "Is there a message to go along with the card?"

"The card is the message. Please make sure Lord Theron receives it." Smiling my thanks, I glance briefly at the darkness in the corner, then head out the door.

Next on my agenda, I need to find a place to stay.

AFTER LIVING IN A POCKET DIMENSION FOR OVER THREE hundred years, with only the occasional visit to the land of the Fae or the Underworld, I quickly realize book learning is not a substitute for experience. It's one thing to read and imagine a massive city like this one, but it's quite another to walk the pavement with hundreds of others, while skyscrapers tower over you.

A cacophony of sounds and smells assault me as I walk towards the hotel. The familiar sounds of laughter, a crying baby, and barking dogs fill the air, until the jarring sounds of car horns and roaring trains replace the familiar with the new.

My stomach rumbles with hunger as I pass a couple of restaurants. I breathe in deeply, trying to inhale more of the delicious aroma, but unfortunately, I pick up a few smells belonging to the city itself—mustiness from old buildings, trash on the curbs, and a strong smell emanating from the sewer. With a wrinkle, I hold my breath until I get farther down the block.

Amazingly, humans and supernaturals exist side-by-side in this bustling city, all of them going about their busy lives, paying scant attention to the person or being next to them. It's remarkable and a testament to the determination of both sides to co-exist. There are only a handful of these cities in the world, the rest dedicated to either supernatural or human, not both. Witches, who are both human and supernatural, reside in cities like this one. In fact, Witchwood, their headquarters, is in this city. It's one reason I'm here.

Following the directions to the hotel, I engage in a brief game of I Spy. *Shifter, incubus, human, chaos demon, witch, unknown supernatural, Fae...*

My cell phone rings, startling me because I'm still not used to having one. "Hello?"

"Hello. Lord Theron is available to meet you at three p.m. today at The Abbey," the woman from earlier states flatly, then hangs up.

Glancing at the phone, I notice it's about noon. Plenty of time to get lunch and check into my hotel.

AFTER CHECKING IN, I ORDER ROOM SERVICE AND GRAB A shower. Exhaustion wears heavily on me, but this meeting is critical to my plans, so I shrug it off. Similar to this morning, I plan my outfit carefully. Too casual is an affront to the aristocratic

Fae, which means jeans are out, and too dressy screams desperation. Sorting through the closet, I finally settle on an outfit and dress quickly.

I sweep critical eyes over my reflection in the mirror. The Fae can be excruciatingly particular about appearances and cruel to those unable to meet their impossibly high standards. It's a balance. I don't want my appearance to be a distraction, nor do I want to be dismissed, either.

At five foot eleven, I'm pretty tall, but adding my favorite pair of silver high heels brings me up to a noticeable six foot two. My long legs are encased in perfectly creased black dress pants, which I've topped with a silky green blouse to bring out the green in my hazel eyes. My makeup is subtle, and my blonde hair, styled in loose waves, frames my face. The overall impression is elegance and sophistication, and I nod in satisfaction.

Now for the hard part. With a deep breath, I slowly spool my magic down deep until its power level registers as moderate. Sweat dots my forehead when I'm finished, but it's necessary. I don't know who's going to be at the club, and my power level needs to remain a secret for now, even from Lord Theron.

I roll my shoulders to ease the tension. Given the tight rein on my power, I'll need to disperse small quantities of magic frequently to maintain control. Hopefully, the wards around the club could use a boost of magic.

Twenty minutes later, I enter The Abbey and walk towards the bar. Unlike earlier, soft ambient lighting has replaced the darkness, highlighting the woman behind the bar. Tilting my head, I consider the picture in front of me.

Déjà vu? No, just the usual Fae tricks, I muse.

Without the slightest hesitation, I walk up to the bar and study the beautiful Fae standing there. Apparently, he likes to use his mastery of illusion to fool unsuspecting witches, but unfortunately for him, I've been living with a powerful Fae for a long time and the illusion is pretty ineffective on me.

I can't say the same about him, though. Fae are beautiful, elegant beings. I've been around them all of my life, and I'd have sworn I had an immunity to them, until him. This man is the perfect embodiment of their best traits and I'm quite sure he knows it, but I can't help my reaction.

His hand-tailored navy pinstripe suit is impeccable on his tall, muscular body. Golden blond hair lies perfectly on top of his pale symmetrical face, while violet eyes, framed with long dark eyelashes, stare impassively at me. The tilt of his head and the tiniest smirk on his face display a hint of arrogance and superiority, hallmarks of the Fae.

I take a deep breath and inhale the most delicious scent—dark chocolate and...winter, like a cool, crisp peppermint covered in creamy decadence.

His power...I shiver. The power emanating from him calls to me. Power likes power, and mine wants nothing more than to reach out and tangle with his. Tingles race over me, and my body heats in response.

Interesting...I acknowledge as we continue to study each other.

His eyes sweep over me, lingering for a moment on the rune tattooed on my throat, before continuing down to the tips of my toes. A glint appears in his eyes, but it's gone when I blink. Then again, it could have been a trick of the light.

The Fae are extremely good at politics, due to their inherent ability to bluff. Emotions, too easily displayed by shifters, humans, and other races, are ruthlessly controlled by the Fae, which means you usually can't tell how a Fae is feeling unless you're a trusted part of their inner circle or they deign to tell you.

My message must be incredibly important to him. I watch his fingers tap restlessly at his side, betraying his nervousness. Of course, he still thinks I can't see him.

Stepping close, I bow my head in acknowledgement of his

aristocratic status. "Hello, Lord Theron. Thank you for meeting with me." Laughing silently, I wait for him to drop the illusion.

Startled, he immediately stops tapping and waves a hand to disperse the illusion. "Good evening." He dips his chin in return. After all, he would never bow to anyone except royalty. "A witch carrying a message from the Princess of the Light Fae? You have my complete and undivided attention. Who are you, and how do you come to possess this message?" His voice is low, perfectly modulated and formal. How the Fae love formality, and given the immaculate vision in front of me, I'm guessing he excels at it.

Such arrogance. I sigh inwardly with exasperation and amusement. Smiling, I hold out my hand and introduce myself. "Arden, House of the Princess of the Light Fae and Vargas Karth." Waiting for my words to sink in, I watch his eyes widen infinitesimally. "Is there somewhere private we can talk?"

2

ARDEN

He motions to the left, where a bank of elevators sits silently waiting. Using a light touch on my back, he guides me towards them. We enter and, using a voice laced with power, he commands the elevator to take us to his office. Feeling the tingle of magic, I raise my brow in wonder. I hadn't seen an elevator shaft, and given the shift sideways, I highly doubt we're moving directly up and down. I marvel at the combination of technology and magic used to operate the elevator.

Pressure builds and surrounds me, pressing into my pores and swirling through the air, searching for the door to my magic and secrets. I strengthen my walls, resisting his invasion, but with my magic repressed, it's a tough battle. The power he's throwing towards me is suffocating, and it's all I can do to control my magic and keep it locked down. It's easy to see why he's part of the Imperium Cadre with this amount of magic at his disposal. Sweat dots my forehead, which he notes with satisfaction. I grit my teeth, aggravated I can't give him a taste of his own medicine, but it's imperative he believes my power is of little consequence.

"How did you come to be part of the House of Light and Karth?" he demands, his voice even, despite the power he's wielding.

"Solandis is my guardian," I reply shortly, without elaborating.

His head whips towards me. "You dare to call the Princess of the Light Fae by her given name?"

Despite a desperate need to roll my eyes, I maintain my composure. Barely. "It's not her given name, as you well know. It's the name she gives to her *close* family and friends." Arching a brow, I shift to face him more directly.

His eyes glint briefly with appreciation at my knowledge. The Fae would never give their true name to anyone, as it holds power over them. "Close, huh? How did a witch become *close* to the Princess of the Light Fae, much less her ward?"

Pressing my lips together, I state, "It's not important right now. Solandis is requesting a favor, and in return, she will absolve your life debt."

Shock emanates from him, and his power retreats. "The entire life debt?"

While I want to sink to the floor with relief, I don't give him the satisfaction. Steeling my shoulders straight, I pull out a thick cream envelope embossed with her official seal and hand it to him. "The details are in the letter."

Palming the envelope, he turns towards the front of the elevator as the doors conveniently open. "My office is this way. We'll have absolute privacy in there."

Stepping out into a small but empty foyer, I notice a black door to my left.

What is it with all the black doors around here?

Lord Theron places his palm on the door while murmuring

an incantation. The door opens quietly. "The combination of technology and magic you use for operations and security is astounding. I'd love to learn more about it."

He glances at me but doesn't reply. Sighing, I follow him down the hall and into his office.

It's exactly what I'd expect from a Fae lord. Every piece of material in the room is organic, beautiful, and immaculate. A wood desk with raw edges sits squarely in the middle of the room, a black, tufted wool chair behind it and two luxurious green silk chairs in front. A gorgeous but muted cream and black wool rug sits beneath the desk and chairs. Matching wood shelves line the walls, books standing side by side like soldiers in a military lineup. Not one item is out of place, and not one iota of dust covers any surface.

Motioning me to a chair, he walks around, sits behind the desk, and pulls out the letter. While I wait for him to read the contents, I peruse the titles on the bookshelves. *Fae Mythology*, *Ancient Fae Discoveries*, *The Harmony of Technology and Magic*.

Hmm...I might have to borrow the last one.

Moments later, he drops the letter on the desk and stares at me. I can almost see the thoughts racing through his mind. If I could guess, I'm sure it would be something along the lines of, *What's so important about this girl? Will the Princess of the Light Fae really absolve me of my life debt? What am I missing?* I wait patiently for him to come to the conclusion he's going to help me.

"Let me get this straight. You need a job, magical training, and help in uncovering your past, correct?" He waits for my confirmation. "The favor hardly seems worth my life debt. I'm a Fae lord, and heir to two different courts. You're a witch, a human, with moderate power. She could have asked for one of my kingdoms, given the magnitude of saving my life, but since she's a princess, she doesn't need a kingdom. She needs something only I can provide, right?" He ponders. "My two greatest advantages are this sanctuary and the power of my cadre. Which do you need?"

Staring at him steadily, I give him no additional clues. This is not a negotiation. "So does that mean you'll help me in exchange for your life debt? It might take time and effort to uncover my past."

His eyes are intense as they stare into mine. Finally, he answers, "Yes, I'll honor this favor."

Relief at his response pours through me, but I don't let one ounce of it show. "I look forward to working here, training with your team, and researching my past."

"My team? You mean the cadre?" He blinks. "I don't think we need to involve them for a witch of your power. We should be able to get a decent witch to train you."

"No witches," I tell him, irritation tightening my voice.

He picks up the letter again to reread the details. "It says I need to provide you with a qualified trainer suitable to your needs."

Irritation sweeps through me at his response. Essentially, in Fae terms, it means he's going to do what he thinks is best. "Fine," I reply curtly. I'll find a way around it later.

Tapping the letter, he outlines our next steps. "Let's go down and talk to Maya. She's the manager of The Abbey, and I believe you met earlier. She'll give you an interview and figure out where we can put you to work. In the meantime, I'll work on setting up a training facility and a trainer."

A job, something I've always wanted. I've trained tirelessly my entire life, physically, emotionally, and mentally preparing for my "destiny." A job is normal wrapped in a pink bow with a unicorn on top. Excitement thrums through me.

I calmly follow him out the door, wanting so badly to sigh loudly in relief at passing this first hurdle, but I don't dare. I need answers, and this is the first step towards finding them.

3

THERON

Standing in the shadows, I watch Arden's interview with Maya. She exhibits grace and a maturity I rarely see in young witches. Usually, they're arrogant with power and eager to test the strength of their magic. I watch the light play on her hair and listen to her voice as she answers Maya's questions. On the surface, she looks and feels exactly how she appears—a beautiful witch, mid-twenties, moderate power level. And yet, my gut clenches as the winds of change blow through me.

Air displaces on my left, and a cool voice sneers, "We're giving jobs to witches now?"

"The Princess of the Light Fae called in a favor," I reply, turning to the vampire beside me. "I'm to provide her with a job, magical training, and some research."

Daire turns towards the girl. Cocking his head to the right, he studies her. "The princess, huh? She's hardly important.

Moderate power. Human. An easy favor. What's the benefit to you?" With a shrug, he turns back to me for my answer.

"A life debt absolved," I murmur. I let a tiny frown show to convey my concern.

Shock covers his expression. "What the fuck? That's an insignificant request for a debt of that magnitude."

I turn to face the witch and admit, "I accepted the favor. The burden of this life debt has been weighing on me for almost three hundred years. I can't help but feel I'm being played, though. There are too many inconsistencies popping up."

Facing me, he crosses his arms. "Like what?"

"Despite being mid-level, she immediately saw through my illusion," I say, thinking back to our introduction. "When I probed, she resisted all my attempts to break through her barriers. And the rune tattoo on her throat makes me feel as if I'm missing an important detail."

"Interesting. I didn't see the rune earlier," he muses.

"Earlier? When did you see her?" I question.

"When she delivered the card, I was walking to the bar for a drink," he says. "Then I got a whiff of her, and I stopped."

"And?" I ask impatiently.

He licks his lips. "She smelled divine. Like a bouquet of my favorite flavors wrapped up in one delicious package." Pausing, he contemplates his next words. "Funny thing, though, I could have sworn she felt me in the room. As she was leaving, she looked directly into the shadows where I was standing."

Vampires are near impossible to detect, except by the most powerful. My shoulders tense as the inconsistencies continue to add up. Normally, I thrive in tackling the unknown, uncovering secrets and delving deep until I solve the puzzle. A slight tremor of unease runs through me. If I wasn't so confident in the integrity of the Princess of the Light Fae, I wouldn't have accepted the favor so easily. Now, I'm wondering if my faith is misplaced.

"She's under my protection, and therefore, the cadre's. Please refrain from drinking her blood, no matter how good she smells." I pause for a second to let my words sink in. "I'll inform Fallon and the rest of the team. For now, we'll monitor her while we meet the terms of the requested favor. Personally, I'm going to make sure she causes as little disruption to our life as possible."

Amused, he reads the uneasiness on my face. "Easy enough. Solange would be impossible if I drank from a witch." He shudders with mock horror. "You better warn Astor personally. She's a tempting morsel, and he rarely denies himself." With those final words and one last glance at Arden, he vanishes.

She is a tempting morsel indeed, reminding me of the beautiful Amazon warriors of the past. I make a note to talk to Astor immediately, turning my head back to Arden just in time to watch her shake Maya's hand.

Maya's voice rings out as she states, "Welcome to The Abbey. Please be here early tomorrow, and we'll get you set up in the system. Uniform comprises a black tank top or T-shirt, which we'll provide, and any black pants or skirt of your choosing."

4

ARDEN

When I return the next evening, the club is buzzing with activity as employees rush to set up prior to opening. Maya is standing at the end of the bar, talking to the bartender. It's another shifter, with golden eyes similar to hers. He sneers in my direction, and Maya turns around to face me. Her eyes sweep over my attire and gleam with satisfaction at the neat appearance of The Abbey tank top, slim black ankle pants, and black tennis shoes.

"Hello, Arden. Let's get started, shall we? I'll introduce you to a few of the staff, give you a brief tour of the club, and then hand you off to Merindah, who will train you for the next week. Okay?" Without waiting for my reply, Maya takes off.

I fall in quickly beside her as she heads toward the back of the club.

"We'll start with the kitchen. This is where you will spend a large majority of your time getting food and non-alcoholic drinks like soda, blood, and other beverages."

"Blood?" I raise an eyebrow at this unexpected beverage.

"Yes, we have vampires and other creatures who prefer blood over more mundane beverages or alcohol. Is it a problem for you?" She smirks as if she thinks it might be.

"No, I simply forgot I'm in mixed company now," I assure her.

She pauses, looks at me in confusion, then shrugs it off and continues, "That is the chef, Syn." She points to a huge man in the corner. The first thing I notice is his long, beautiful hair, in shades of gold and red, pulled back into a ponytail. He turns at Maya's words and flashes his golden eyes towards me. Dipping his chin in acknowledgement, he goes back to his conversation with the staff.

"I'll warn you now. He's a lion shifter and temperamental about his food. If you let a dish get cold or drop one, he's liable to roar. Be respectful of the prepared food and his staff, and you'll get along fine. If not," she shrugs, "then you face the consequences. Also, he's my husband, so you'd better have a legitimate grievance if you complain to me." With that bomb, she heads over to the drink station.

Following her, I swallow and glance back at the man in the corner, only to catch his golden eyes assessing me. Given they're married, I'm sure he's heard about my introduction to The Abbey. I bow my head slightly and turn back to listen to Maya's instructions on how and where to get specific drinks.

"Okay, I know you won't retain all of this today, but once you start serving, you'll get the hang of it. Now, let's go to the bar so I can explain the different types of alcohol we serve." She hurries out the door, and I follow.

As I rush through the door, I collide with a brick wall disguised as a man. A gorgeous man, with dark auburn hair, deep brown eyes, a healthy tan, and a smattering of freckles across his cheeks, as if he spends all his available time outdoors. A light scruff covers his jaw, while pouty lips curved in a smile completes the charming picture. "Oomph, sorry," he says as he straightens and steps back. His eyes rove from my face to my boobs to my legs, checking me out. He smiles broadly. "Well, hello, gorgeous. I don't believe we've met. What's your name?"

He might look like he lives in the sun, but his aura is dark and compelling, and so is the magic stroking against my barriers. I grasp my power with metaphorical fists and hold tightly as it strains to meet his. "Arden," I reply absentmindedly. My brain is busy sifting through his magic, trying to find an answer to what type of being he might be and why he feels so familiar.

With my reply, his eyes cool and narrow briefly, then he flashes his smile again. The smile, calculated and cold, never reaches his eyes, making me shiver, as if the sun dipped behind a cloud. "Arden, yes, I've heard all about you. Welcome to The Abbey. I'm Astor." He inclines his head and steps around me to continue through the kitchen door without waiting for my reply.

Raising my eyebrow, I consider his words. Astor, half warlock, half incubus, and member of the Imperium Cadre. I guess Lord Theron told the rest of his team about me. That's good, since the sooner they get used to me, the better. Although, it seems like Astor is going to avoid me.

"Arden, are you coming?" Maya asks curtly. She's standing by the bar, waving a menu at me.

Hurrying over, I give her an apology and wait for her to walk through the drink menu.

"We offer all the usual cocktails and alcohol," she explains as she lists the various drinks. "Outside of the usual, we offer demon brews, Fae elixirs, Elven wine, shifter moonshine, spiked blood, and a myriad of other specialty liquors preferred by various races. They're listed on the back side of the menu, here." She points to a long, two-column list on the back of the menu.

Familiar with both demon brews and Fae elixirs, I peruse the list and make a note of the more unfamiliar items, like troll tonga and unicorn tears. I'll ask my trainer, Merindah, for more information later.

Maya glances up from the menu and nods to someone behind me.

When I turn around, a petite Fae female, with a long silver ponytail, is standing behind me. I take in each of her symmetrical, delicate features and find her perfect. She's an immaculate pocket Venus. She's dressed similar to me, with a black Abbey tank, a short flirty black skirt, and cute black boots, so I assume she's also an employee.

Bright, turquoise eyes stare up at me, piercing in their intensity as she assesses me. It feels like she's peering into my soul, stripping away all my layers to uncover my deepest secrets and weaknesses. The one other time I've felt this unnerving scrutiny, I was in the Queen of the Light Fae's company. In fact, if I didn't know any better, I'd swear they were related. The turquoise eyes are so similar, it's uncanny.

"Merindah, this is Arden. Arden, as I mentioned previously, Merindah will be your trainer for the next week. Listen and follow her lead. She's excellent at her job, and the customers love her. I'll leave you in her capable hands. We'll regroup at the end of the week and see how things are going, okay?" Without waiting for my reply, she waves at the bartender and hurries over to point at the shelf behind him.

I smile and hold out my hand in a gesture of polite formality. When she shakes my hand, I jump at the sheer power I feel coursing through her.

Hell, make that a powerhouse pocket Venus.

"Hi, Merindah. It's nice to meet you, and I appreciate your agreeing to train me this week," I say enthusiastically.

"You're exceptionally powerful," she replies abruptly. "But for some reason, you're hiding it. Why?"

Shocked, I glance around to see if anyone heard her. "Shh. How can you tell? I thought I was hiding it pretty well."

"I sort of see powers," she admits, shrugging.

"And I could say the same about you! You're packing a hell of a lot of power, too. I've not known many Fae with your level of power," I murmur, not wanting anyone to hear. An icy Fae male pops into my head for a second.

"Hmm…yes, sort of," she returns quietly. A light trance glazes her face, eliminating all animation. In a monotone voice, she says, "Secrets and shadows surround you, danger and death desire you, destiny stalks you. When seven and five appear, your role becomes clear. Be wary of the powers who await the chosen breathlessly." With a shake of her head, she stops and smiles.

Shit, she's a seer, but why is she smiling? "Thanks, I think. I've heard a similar obscure vision previously, but that's why I'm here. I'm hoping the cadre can help me. It's a long story, though. One I'm not comfortable sharing yet," I tell her hesitantly. "Why are you smiling?"

"We share a destiny," she muses. "Unknown, with hidden paths, but tied together. I guess we'll both see what happens."

"Well, since that's the case, perhaps you can keep all this to yourself? I'm not asking you to lie, of course, but can you avoid answering questions about me?" I bite my lip, waiting for her answer. Fae can't lie, but they can keep secrets, if they choose, by not volunteering the information to anyone.

Her head tilts as she scrutinizes me. "It will come out sooner rather than later, now you've found the cadre," she draws out slowly, "but I won't be the one to tell anyone here. Now, let's get started." Her turquoise eyes dance as if she's privy to the secrets of the universe.

She shows me to a group of tables on the left side of the dance floor. "We'll be waiting on the customers at these tables tonight." Taking a damp cloth, she wipes them down and places clean menus in the center.

"So, what's up with the dance floor? Why does it look like a spotlight is on it?" I motion over to the glittery dance floor, where the single light still shines. "I assume it's magic, but what's its purpose?"

She grins. "It's definitely magic. When the DJ is playing, the spotlight shines according to the music. On Friday and Saturdays, different races perform. They sing and dance, but it's not fun and games. It's a serious competition with races vying for recognition and coveted prizes. The spotlight coordinates with their choreography."

My brow wrinkles as I try to understand what she's saying. "Why?" Singing or dancing in front of a group of people sounds like a nightmare to me.

"Just because this is a sanctuary doesn't mean they drop all rivalry at the door. This provides the races with a way to express themselves and battle each other without physically fighting. Plus, if they're noticed by one of the cadre, they gain serious bragging rights and tokens of appreciation." Her sigh is wistful as she describes past performances. "Anyway, we've got our first customers. Come on."

Following her over to the table in the corner, I notice it's filled with a group of demons. Dismay fills me when I see Vargas' lieutenant staring at me. I flick my eyes over each of the others, but thankfully, I don't recognize any of them.

"Hello, welcome to The Abbey. How are you doing this evening?" Merindah asks, setting down cocktail napkins. "My name is Merindah, and this is Arden. She's training with me this week. What can we get for you?" As each demon orders, she types in their drink and food orders on her tablet.

The lieutenant drags his eyes from mine. "I'll have Hellfire Brew."

"Great, we'll have your drinks out in a few minutes and get your food ordered," Merindah tells them.

My gaze still on the lieutenant, I plead with him silently not to say anything to anyone about my being here. Walking away, I pull out my phone and send a quick text message to Vargas, then hurry to catch up with Merindah.

She's standing by the bar waiting for me. "It's pretty fast-paced around here, so please try to keep up. We punch in their order directly into the tablet." Showing me the tablet, she explains the ordering system, which is pretty straightforward and fast. "The food will take a few minutes, but since it's not busy, the drinks should be ready by now."

The bartender sets down several drinks, along with a smile for Merindah and another sneer towards me. What is his problem with me? It's the second time I've noticed it. I turn my head and focus on Merindah.

After checking the ticket to make sure it's our order, she picks up a tray. "You always use a tray to deliver the drinks. It takes practice to get used to it, but it saves time because you can carry more drinks." Holding the tray in her left hand, she uses her right hand to load the drinks onto the tray. "Be sure to start by placing drinks in the middle of the tray and adjust the balance as you add more drinks. A tray will usually hold about eight drinks, give or take." She turns and strides off towards the table, with me trailing behind her.

She hands each drink to me, and I set them down in front of the appropriate person. As I set down the last drink, a meaty purple hand reaches out and grabs my wrist. "I ordered Hellfire Brew."

Running through the order in my head, I disagree. "You ordered Hell's Breath."

Enraged, he stands up and bellows, "I ordered Hellfire Brew. Are you calling me a liar?"

Merindah opens her tablet. "Sir, this tablet automatically records your order. I can play it back if you like?" Without waiting for his reply, she punches play. His voice rings out clearly. "Hell's Breath."

His friends bust out laughing when he's called out. He glares at them, sits down, and gulps down his drink. Letting out a burp in my face, he demands, "Now, I'll have a Hellfire Brew. Did you record my order in your tiny device?"

Waving my hand at the smell, I look over at Merindah. She gives him a tiny scowl of her own and hits play on the tablet. This time, his voice rings out with, "Hellfire Brew."

Spinning on her heel, she walks over to another table of customers sitting down. After greeting them, we get their drink orders, then head towards the kitchen.

"Damn chaos demons," I grit out. "Always trying to cause trouble."

She laughs. "They hate the recorder. Some servers don't like to use them, but it saves us a lot of aggravation."

Grinning, I tell her, "I'm surprised we're allowed to use one."

"The Abbey sets its own rules. If they don't agree, they're not welcome here," she explains bluntly as we enter the kitchen.

"I'm definitely going to use one," I mutter, still irritated with the asshole demon.

The kitchen is controlled chaos as orders are shouted out and handed off to servers. We step up to get the food onto our trays, then head back to the table of demons. On the way, Merindah picks up the additional pint of Hellfire Brew.

Setting down the food and drink, the demon crew devours it while simultaneously shouting out orders for refills. The slight chaos sets the tone for the entire night. We run from table to table, serving all kinds of beings. I get my first introduction to trolls, big, hairy men who are as sweet as sugar, and gargoyles, loud and boisterous instead of stoic like I expected. And stacked with muscle. Who knew gargoyles were so sexy?

After receiving a text message from Vargas, the lieutenant stopped staring at me and the tension eased from my shoulders. I know my location will leak out soon, but until I can start my magical training, I don't want others to know.

By the end of the night, I'm exhausted, but Merindah tells me it will get even busier as we get closer to the weekend. "You did well tonight and will be waiting tables on your own by next week," she reassures me. She hesitates a second, then continues, "Here, this might help you. I'll see you tomorrow night. Oh, and Arden…feel free to call me Meri."

I glance down at the book she gave me. A book she pulled out of thin air, I might add. *Witch Heritage: The Founding Families.* I run my hands over the embossed cover and flip carefully through its pages. The heavy tome is musty, its pages brittle, speaking of its age. I've been looking for this book for a long time. I can't help but wonder where she found it. Clutching it to me, I hurry out the door, ready to get home and start reading.

5

ARDEN

By Friday, I'm successfully waiting on tables with Merindah's supervision. She's a fantastic trainer and really nice, too. If it wasn't for her, I don't know if I'd have survived working at The Abbey. Many of the staff are not happy about working with a witch. Several hide behind a polite mask, while others, like the bartender, openly sneer at me. Sometimes, I have to wait longer for my drinks or my order is mysteriously messed up, but they're minor things. Thankfully, Maya keeps a tight rein on her staff, so nobody has physically assaulted me or anything.

As a witch who's been hiding for over three hundred years, I didn't realize witches have a reputation for being greedy and supremely entitled, with a shocking habit of using magic to manipulate the world, and the supes, around them.

A sweep of air and Merindah steps in behind me. "Hi, Arden. Tonight is going to be crazy busy. We'll serve the tables together tonight, then tomorrow night, I'll give you a couple of tables of your own, okay?" she tosses over her shoulder as she hurries to prep the tables.

I jump in to help finish the rest. "Hi, Merindah," I respond, laughing. She rarely waits for me. If she's talking, she's usually moving. Fast. "That sounds great." I wonder if I'll see any other witches tonight. So far, the only witch I've seen lately is the one in the mirror each morning.

By ten p.m., the club is hopping, vibrant with beings from all races. Dressed to impress and seduce, they prowl and glide their way around each other. Shifters, vampires, elves, and many more. They all come to The Abbey to play.

Shifters, like our manager, Maya, are harder to distinguish. Merindah explained Maya is the alpha of her lion pride. I could tell she was a shifter, but not what type. Unfortunately, unless you can recognize their unique scent or specific characteristics, you likely won't know until they tell or show you.

Our first table gets seated, and it's a table of shifters. I glance at Merindah, and she mouths "wolves" to me as we walk up to greet them and take their order. I'm not sure if she automatically knows or has the "nose."

They all order drinks, so we head towards the bar to pick them up. The bar is packed, and it takes a few minutes to get the drinks. In the meantime, another table is seated. It's a group of ladies, but I can't tell their race from here.

Merindah hands me a tray, and we load them up with the drinks for the wolves. Heading back over, I notice the table of ladies are witches. My hands tremble at the thought of meeting them, and a few drops of beer spill over the top of the mug.

"Hey, watch it. If you spill anymore, you'll be buying me another drink," a dark-haired wolf snarls at me.

"Sorry," I murmur, hurriedly wiping up the spilt beer. Putting the napkin in my apron, I turn to walk away when a hand reaches out and slaps my ass.

What the hell?!

Merindah steps up, saving the guy from my wrath. "Unless she asks you to smack her ass, don't," she warns him, "or you can explain to the cadre why you have the manners of an ass instead of a wolf."

The entire table laughs as they make burn noises.

"Oooh, burn, man," one guy crows.

"Shut up, fucker!" the guy who smacked my ass yells back at him. He turns to me and glowers but says nothing.

"Wonderful. Glad we have that all cleared up," Merindah states dryly. "Let us know when you're ready for another round." Grabbing my arm, she pulls me toward the table of witches.

Merindah holds her stylus, ready for their order. "Good evening, I'm Merindah and this is Arden. We'll be waiting on you ladies tonight. What can we get for you?"

They look up to order and pause when they notice me. Shock chases away their laughter quickly as they realize I'm a witch, too. Instead of greeting me, everyone pivots to face the blonde woman in the middle, as if she's their leader.

Placing her palms on the table, the blonde stands slowly, then the rest of the witches stand with her. "Who are you?" she asks tersely. "Where did you come from?"

"I'm Arden, pleased to meet you," I reply, holding out my hand. "And you are?"

She ignores my hand to state, "I'm Cassandra Pennington, of course, the most powerful witch in existence with five bloodlines. These are my friends and fellow coven witches, Essa, Natasha, and my sister, Charlotte. My mother is Caro Pennington, leader of the light witches and ruler of the witches' council. We know every witch, but we don't know you. Who are you?"

"I'm Arden," I repeat, puzzled at the question.

"Are you stupid or plain ignorant? I mean, what bloodline are you? Who are your parents?" she grits out angrily.

"I don't understand the question about bloodline," I explain. "As to my parents..." I shrug as if I don't know the answer to that question, either. Technically, I know who my mother is, but the information is need to know. And given my mother's explicit instructions to stay away from witches for most of my life, I'll keep the information to myself for a while.

"I'm sorry to interrupt an all-powerful witch like yourself," Merindah butts in with a subtle sneer, "but we need to take your order and get to our other tables. If not, Maya is going to get upset and come over here." She jerks her head towards the bar, where Maya stands, staring at us.

The blonde tosses her hair back and sits down before demanding snidely, "We'll take a couple of bottles of Chardonnay and clean glasses."

The rest follow her lead and sit. A couple of them whisper behind their hands as they stare at me.

I give them all one last look, then follow Merindah to the next table. Thankfully, this table is full of vampires. After taking their order for spiked blood, we rush to the bar to grab drinks.

We set down the vampire orders and move on to the witches. Setting down the two bottles of wine in ice buckets, we distribute the glasses. Walking away, I hear my name called.

"Arden, is it?" Cassandra asks with a smile. "We'd like to order a few appetizers."

Pulling up my tablet, I stand by to get their order, while Merindah goes to check on the wolves. "Absolutely, what would you like?"

"We'll take the hummus with pita chips and the spinach and artichoke dip," she replies before laughter spills out of her. "Sorry, I shouldn't laugh. I simply can't get over the novelty of a witch working."

"I enjoy working," I comment, while jotting down her order in the tablet. I give her a brief smile in return and ignore her laughter. Maybe she needs a few minutes to get over the shock of meeting an unknown witch. I mean, they can't know every witch in the supernatural universe, right? "Your food should be ready in about fifteen minutes."

Turning my back, I sweep the area for Merindah and find her standing by the bar. As I walk towards her, a hand comes out and slaps my ass...again.

Seriously? What are we, fucking twelve? I huff angrily and zap his hand. I glare down at him, waiting for his response.

"What the fuck?! You witch bitch!" he yells, surging to his feet.

"The next time you put your hand on my ass, I'll set it on fire. Got it, asshole?" I bite out as I look up at him. He's got at least six inches on me, but I've beaten bigger. Sounds die down around us, and I distribute my weight in anticipation. He snarls and clenches his fists.

"Tsk, tsk, tsk. Now, Jason, what have I told you about putting your hands on our staff?" a familiar dark voice rings out behind me, and the air stirs with the smell of burnt cedar and sex.

I shuffle to the side until I can see both the wolf and the person behind me. Astor stands there with his hands on his hips, a small smile gracing his lips. He looks amused until you see the darkness swirling in his eyes. Shadows from the blackest corners of sanctuary slide up and surround him.

"Since when do you care about witches?" The wolf snorts, and the crowd laughs.

"When the witch works for The Abbey." Astor's voice is mild as he explains, but a hint of possessiveness enters his tone. "We don't allow anyone to mess with our employees. You know the rules. Unless provoked, you'll be punished according to the offense."

The wolf nervously blurts out, "She zapped me!"

Astor cocks an eyebrow towards me.

I roll my eyes and shrug. "He's slapped my ass twice tonight. The first time, Merindah gave him a nice verbal warning. Obviously, it didn't penetrate his thick skull. I figured a little pain might work better. Maybe I shouldn't have been so lenient."

Fury darkens Astor's face, and with a simple hand gesture, he creates a window behind us and sends the shifter flying out. Where he lands is unknown. It depends on how far Astor threw him. Before the window closes, Astor snarls at the wolf's companions. "Are you leaving the easy way or the hard way?" he demands.

The rest of the wolves scramble up and head out the door. The DJ starts up the music, and the sounds from the crowd ramp up again.

"I can take care of myself," I tell him, irritated with his interference.

"I'm sure you can, gorgeous," he replies with smoky laughter, "but why don't you leave the magic to someone better?" Wrapping his arm around a nearby brunette in a skimpy dress, he strolls off to the VIP area.

Scowling, I watch him retreat and stomp over to Merindah. My magic burns to show him exactly what I can do. Prick.

Merindah throws an arm around me. "You can knock him on his ass next week, okay?"

"Promise?" I grin, picturing it.

"Absolutely," she reassures me. "I never lie."

"Hmm, definitely Fae," I tease.

"One hundred percent," she admits, an almost bitter tone in her voice.

"You know, you remind me of the Queen of the Light Fae," I say, although I don't tell her she looks enough like her to be her daughter.

"You know the queen?" she asks quietly. When I nod, she thinks for a second. "Did you meet her when you won the Gathering of the Light?" She points to the rune at my throat.

Pursing my lips, I study her for a second. "How did you know?"

"I recognize the work of the queen's Rune Master, Rivan," she says, before pulling back her hair to show me the small rune tattooed behind her ear.

I start to ask about her rune, but someone shouts, "Can we order drinks?!" and we're off running again.

Midnight rolls around, and The Abbey is packed. As we set down drinks at one of our tables, the lights flicker, and the ladies in the club scream with excitement. Whistles ring out from the males. Merindah swings by and grabs my arm, pulling me to the dance floor.

"What's going on?" I yell, trying to be heard above the crowd.

"A group is going to perform," she replies, waving at the dance floor. "The lights flicker to signal the first performance, and everything stops so we can all watch."

The lights dim around us until a single spotlight shows in the middle of the dance floor. The first bars of Camila Cabello's "My Oh My" start, and five incubi appear in a shimmer on the dance floor. With the clap in the beginning chorus of the music, five blonde females appear in their arms, and the dance begins.

The incubi are inhumanly beautiful as they command their equally seductive partners around the dance floor. The song is a mix of playfulness and sensuality, perfect for the incubi's natural showmanship. I'm mesmerized by their allure and grace as I watch their bodies move in sync to the tempo. While the crowd laughs at the dancers' expressions, their bodies unconsciously sway to the beat, while incubus magic, a tangible essence, permeates the air, heating their blood.

A dark symphony of desire and laughter swirls through me, and my body throbs in response. Laughing, I spin and dance sensually with the others in the crowd, the tension from the last week dissipating as the performance works its magic. I throw my head back and find myself ensnared by a pair of smoky brown eyes, staring down at me from above. The heat and magic of the dance burns bright, inciting the same desire that fuels my abandonment.

Swaying slightly, I dance for him, holding his attention in my fists, refusing to let his eyes wander. Dark shadows flick lightly along my neck, as if his phantom lips trail down the side. A shadow hand winds itself in my hair, pulling my head back until my neck is exposed, vulnerable to his will. His dark eyes gleam with satisfaction as those phantom lips move down, placing kisses along the way.

I moan. *Two can play that game.*

Using my own metaphysical finger, I trail it lightly across his lips and down his neck to the first button on his shirt. Flicking it open, I caress the warm skin. Another button, another caress. His hand tightens on the railing. I smile at his response and blow him a kiss.

The crowd's sudden clapping and cheering brings me out of my hazy state. Glancing at the dance floor, I realize the incubi have finished their performance and are looking to Astor for approval. He stares down at them, making them wait, before a sinful smile crosses his lips, and he tosses them a gold coin. The crowd roars in approval.

"Why did he pay them?" I ask Merindah. My voice husky from the sensual interlude.

"They won Astor's favor with their performance," she replies thoughtfully. "While he's not the Lord Demon of Incubi, he's part incubus and his status in the Imperium Cadre affords him a prestigious role in the incubi hierarchy. It's been a long time since anyone won Astor's favor. It was an excellent performance, though. Even I felt that one. The incubi must have used a spell to push out so much lust. It was an interesting blend of witch and incubus magic."

*Hmm…*Astor is part incubus and part light witch, so I could see how the blend would appeal to him. My investigation into the cadre revealed he uses spell magic and sex magic equally, much to the delight of the female population. Charming and seductive, he's a natural playboy who holds court in the VIP section every night, with women clamoring to cater to his every whim. Blowing out a breath, I glance up to find him gone. Thank goodness. The last thing I need right now is a distraction.

Rolling my shoulders, I glance over at Merindah and motion to the tables to let her know I'm going to check on them. She waves their bills to let me know they're ready to check out. Thank goodness. I'm so ready to get out of here tonight.

6

ARDEN

Theron: We will hold your first magical training session at The Abbey at noon. Please inform me if this time doesn't work for you.

Arden: That time works for me. Who's conducting the training?

Theron: I asked the witches' council for two of their best trainers.

Arden: …

I put my phone down and blow out an irritated breath. It's not a surprise he's chosen witches for my training. I knew keeping my power under wraps would likely result in a misconception, but until I was sure he would follow through on his agreement, I didn't want to reveal myself. I think it's time, though. As for the witches, I can use this advantage to learn more about my witch power and heritage without revealing myself until I'm ready.

Arriving at The Abbey at ten to noon, I'm patiently waiting by the elevators for him to come get me. The elevator dings and the doors open, but instead of Lord Theron, a beautiful, blond vampire steps out. Not just any vampire, either. The vampire before me, with piercing, ice-blue eyes, is the First Vampire, otherwise known as Daire. He's been given the title First Vampire because he's literally the first of his kind, born to Lucifer and a powerful witch and healer. He's also a Prince of the Underworld and a member of the Imperium Cadre. Three down, two to go.

"Hello, witch. Theron sent me to fetch you to the training room," he sneers, then sweeps his arm towards the elevator.

I'm not sure if he's sneering at my being a witch or because Theron asked him to complete such a lowly task. Standing tall, I stride past him into the elevator.

Upon entering, he murmurs, "Training room." The elevator doors close, and we're moving. Propping himself against the far wall, he crosses his arms and stares at me, making me shiver. A vampire's stare is potent, even when they're not trying to compel you. Given he's the first vampire ever created, his stare is mesmerizing and overwhelmingly sensual, like a predator who lures his victims with tantalizing promises of uninhibited desire.

Heat rises, making me flush, and my heart beats faster. My hand raises involuntarily to stroke his face, but I quickly turn it sideways as if my intent is an introduction. Of course, he promptly ignores it. Lowering my hand, I shrug. "It's nice to meet you, Daire. After hearing about you for years, you're not exactly what I expected," I tease softly. I'm such a liar. Physically, he's exactly the man I envisioned, and I've imagined him a lot since he starred in many of my daydreams growing up. Looking at the panel, I curse my inability to operate the damn elevator by myself.

He bares his teeth in mockery as he asks snidely, "What have you heard about me?"

Tilting my head, I think back to the many conversations I've had about him. "I've heard you're an excellent leader to the vampires. You're a fierce warrior and loyal to your cadre, even saving their lives a time or two. You're arrogant, but not conceited. Although I've never met a vampire who isn't conceited, so that might not be true." Pausing, I bring up my favorite story. "When you were twenty, you saved your half-sister from being stolen by a demon lord and his gang." And became the blond warrior starring in my teenage dreams, slaying bad guys and saving damsels in distress.

Rigid now, he stares at me in shock. A thin layer of blue fire scales the inside of the elevator as his anger rises to the surface. "How the hell do you know so much about me?"

The elevator doors slide open, but he uses his arm to bar me from leaving.

"Your father. He's extremely proud," I confide. "He's been telling me stories about you for years."

He raises a single eyebrow, snorts, then states derisively, "First of all, a lowly witch would never have the ear of my father. Second, my father is interested in feats of power, not acts of loyalty and courage."

"You're wrong, and you're forgetting something." I smile sweetly, ducking under his arm.

"What's that?" he mocks.

"While the princess was my guardian, I lived in the House of Light...and Karth. Vargas Karth's house. You know, Lucifer's executioner?" I remind him as I walk backwards. Seeing the astonishment reflected on his face, I turn around and laugh. "Thanks for the ride."

DOUBLE DOORS AT THE END OF THE HALLWAY LEAD INTO A cavernous training room. By the looks of the equipment and weapons, they dedicated one end of the room to fighting and physical training. And on this end of the room, they enclosed a large space to allow for the safe practice of magic. The "walls" are magical barriers made to absorb and neutralize spells and magic.

Stepping through the barrier, I enter the space and walk towards Lord Theron and the two women standing with him, who I presume to be the witch trainers. Tightening my shields, I stroll up to them and hold out my hand for introductions.

"Hello, I'm Arden," I say and give them my most pleasant smile. Lord Theron would probably look startled if he wasn't Fae, but all I get is the tiniest flicker of one eyebrow. I don't know why he's so surprised. I wasn't raised in a barn. Solandis is a terror for proper manners. As a Princess of the Light Fae, etiquette was a high priority in our house.

"Hello, Arden. I'm Clare Pennington and this is Bianca Perrone. Let's get started, shall we?" She smiles briefly at me, and with a spell, transforms the space around us into a miniature training facility. Tables set with various training objects, including candles, potion ingredients, a grimoire, a map, and other similar items. I feel like I'm five years old again. I turn to give Lord Theron an irritated glance, but he's immersed in his phone.

"I'm not sure all this is necessary. I know the basics," I reassure her.

"That's for us to decide. Besides, these training items test your affinity for specific bloodlines," she replies, motioning me to the first table. "This table tests your elemental abilities. Using fire, air, earth, water, and spirit, you will complete each of the tasks. Instructions are beside each one. We'll grade you on your effort and rate you, according to a predetermined scale, on your affinity to this bloodline. I've got to make a phone call, but Bianca is well qualified to complete the elemental testing."

"Elemental is a bloodline?" I ask while stepping up to the table to read the first card. The instructions state, "Light the candles." Without a thought, I glance at the candles and they light.

"Were you not taught the bloodlines?" Bianca asks, shock in her voice. "Yes, bloodline five is elemental powers."

"My mother died shortly after I was born, and my guardians raised me. They brought tutors in to teach me magic, but none would share any witch knowledge or history with us." I purposely do not mention my guardians were demon and Fae, not witches.

Looking at the second card, it states, "Extinguish the candles." Frustrated, I blow out a breath and direct it towards the candles to extinguish their flames.

"That's odd. The bloodlines are not a secret," she remarks. "There are six bloodlines passed down from the six founding witch families. While witches may have a mix of powers, their strongest affinity is their bloodline. For example, the Peronne family's strongest affinity is to bloodline one, which is mastery of portals and precognition. We've had many seers in our family, including Gia Perrone, the most powerful seer in the last thousand years. I, myself, only experience the occasional vision, but I'm a master in creating portals, with the ability to create them between worlds."

My heart skips a beat. "It's passed down through the families? So, it's a literal representation of the blood and family's power? What are the other bloodlines?" I ask steadily, as if the answers are of no consequence.

Looking down at the third card, I read the instructions. "Make the plant grow." Using a mixture of my magic, earth and water, the plant shoots up through the soil until it stands four feet tall with a multitude of leaves. At the tip of one branch, a brilliant pink and white camellia flower blooms.

"Well, bloodline two is illusion and glamour. Both the ability to magic them and the ability to see through them. Bloodline three is spell casting and shielding. The Pennington family has the strongest affinity to bloodline three. Bloodline four is healing and potions. Bloodline five is elemental powers, bloodline six is transfiguration," she says absentmindedly as she studies my test and writes my performance on her tablet. "There's one more card, dear."

Glancing down, I note the instructions. "Use spirit to direct your thoughts to another witch." There's a hell of a lot more to spirit than telepathy, but sure. *Thank you for telling me about the bloodlines.*

Bianca nods when the words reach her. "It was nice of you to add a camellia to the bush." She motions to the flower. "One of my ancestors planted hundreds of them around the grounds of our estate. I prefer the purple ones, but the April Dawn camellia is pretty, too," she says with a smile, pointing to my pink and white flower.

"They were my mother's favorite flowers," I tell her absent-mindedly as my brain digests the information on the various bloodlines. I've never healed anyone, nor have I transformed into anything. That leaves four bloodlines I know I can master easily and equally. "Can you have an affinity for more than one bloodline?"

"Yes, our most powerful witches have mixed bloodlines and therefore strong affinities to several powers. Clare's niece, Cassandra Pennington, whom you've met, is a mixture of five bloodlines. Another witch, Reyna Martinez, is a mixture of four bloodlines. Over the years, the families intermingled pretty heavily in order to create a powerful witch heritage." She turns the tablet around so I can see my scores, which mean nothing to me since she hasn't explained the rating system. "You did well with elementals, showing a strong affinity for this bloodline."

"Wonderful," I say dryly. "What's the next test?"

"Oh, we conduct one test a day, so the witch's power isn't depleted. We'll come back tomorrow and test you for bloodline one," she explains, packing it all away with a simple incantation. "Clare, are you ready?"

"Coming," Clare responds, telling the person on the phone goodbye. "You did well today. We'll resume testing tomorrow. At the end of the testing, the council will review the results and invite you to a coven induction ceremony, where you'll find out your placement."

"Placement in what?" I ask.

"The coven is a hierarchy of power and bloodlines. Based on the placement, you're given access to money, prestige, power, and the overall benefits of the entire coven. The council will use your scores to place you where you fit the best and can serve the greater good of the entire coven. We'll see you tomorrow. Come along, Bianca."

Lord Theron reappears near the door to escort them out. I give them five minutes to reach the elevator, then let out a long sigh, along with the tight restraint on my power. My magic stretches fully, as if waking from a long nap. It buzzes around the contained room, leaping with joy and crackling with power. Tension eases from my shoulders, and I laugh with sheer happiness at feeling whole again. This room is the first time I've had the option to release my power since arriving in this city. I'm so immersed in the moment, it takes several minutes to realize I'm being watched. Drawing my power to me, I crouch in a defensive position and whirl around to face the threat behind me.

Lord Theron and Astor stand shoulder to shoulder. Lord Theron's eyebrows are drawn together in fury, while Astor's eyes bounce between me and Lord Theron, apparently fascinated with both my power and Lord Theron's blatant display of emotion.

This wasn't how I wanted to tell him, but now he knows, I'm hoping he'll get me the magical training to fit my needs.

"Can I have him?" I ask, pointing to Astor. "And I want to keep the witches, too."

He communicates silently with Astor for a second, then gives me a curt nod. "He's willing to teach you. Why the witches? You're obviously above their power level."

"They have witch knowledge, which I need. I don't want them knowing how powerful I am, though. Not until I'm ready," I explain, not going into detail on why it needs to remain a secret.

"Done," he agrees. Glaring at me, he doesn't move, and I realize he's ready to escort me out.

"I also need to keep up with my defensive and weapons training. Do you have anyone that can spar with me? Someone good?" I hurriedly spit out my request before he can force me out the door.

"I'll ask Valerian," he replies, pinching the bridge of his nose. "Can I escort you out now?"

"Yes, hold on a second," I tell him. Gathering my power, I spool it down into me. It protests for a moment, then slides into a tight ball. Massive tension, due to the effort of containing the power, burns through me. Rolling my shoulders, I force myself to stand up straight. I look over at Lord Theron and raise an eyebrow.

Lord Theron pivots on his heels and strides angrily to the door. "I hope one day this secrecy doesn't come back to bite me in the ass. If it does, you'd better hide. Now, let me escort you out."

Waving to Astor, who flashes me his signature fake dreamy smile, I follow Lord Theron out the door and into the elevator. When the doors close, he shows me how to operate the elevator to get to the training room. Now that I'm going to be here more often, he doesn't want to spend his valuable time escorting me like a child. At least, that's the explanation I get.

"I appreciate your help, I really do. I'm in a precarious position with few people to trust." My voice is soft as I quietly plead for his understanding. "There have been several assassination attempts on my life, and before I announce myself to the world, I need answers. I know it doesn't ease the duplicity, but I hope you can try to understand." The elevator doors open, and I step out.

7

THERON

The seething fury dampens with her words. While I'm still pissed I don't have all the facts at my disposal, I understand the need for secrecy. Power like hers, mine, and the rest of the cadre's is a beacon to everyone from the highest of positions to the lowest. Jealousy, greed, arrogance, and political power all play their part in our supernatural world.

Running my hand over my face, I realize she's going to need every bit of my help and the cadre's. And who the hell is trying to assassinate her? I know she's not likely to tell us much, but we can help mitigate that threat, at least. Working and training at The Abbey certainly cuts down on the opportunities for assassins to reach her. I don't know where she's living, though. Should we move her into the sanctuary? I'm not sure it's the best idea. It's only been the cadre living here for a long time.

Speaking of the cadre, it's time to remove the barriers I placed between them and Arden. While her path isn't clear to us, her need for allies resonates within me. When I was desperate for people to trust, the cadre stepped in and became the army and brotherhood I didn't know I needed. In pure destruction mode, I was headed towards a cliff when they stepped in and saved me. Fallon recognized something in me that matched them, just as I see something in Arden. I'm not inviting her to join the cadre, but at the very least, we can support her with power, magic, strength, and political capital. Standing alone only makes you a bigger target for your enemies.

Pulling out my phone, I text the cadre to let them know we need to meet this evening and discuss Arden. All of them reply with agreement.

The elevator doors open to my office. Entering, I stride over to my desk to find the letter. It includes Solandis' contact information, and after speaking with the cadre, I need to reach out and see if she's willing and able to part with more information.

Reading the Princess of the Light Fae's letter again, I'm seeing the magnitude of her request. She's essentially entrusted me with the safety and care of one of her family. Purpose and determination fill me. This is a favor worthy of a life debt.

BRINGING UP THE VIDEO CONFERENCE, I TAP IN THE CODE TO connect us to Fallon. He's been away on a mission for the light Elven king for three months now. My mouth tightens at the thought of him doing missions for the bastard. He knows how I —hell, how we all feel about these missions, but only he can tell the king to fuck off. It's his father, after all. I'm doubly thankful my own family is pretty cold and indifferent to everything, including me, after seeing how the king manipulates Fallon's love for him.

A chair creaks, and a scowling face appears on the screen. "I don't think I've ever seen that expression on your face. This must be serious," Fallon drawls tiredly.

I'm tempted to erase any trace of emotion from my face, but I don't. They might tease me, but we don't hide things from each other. "It is," I reply, turning to face the rest of the room.

Valerian, Daire, and Astor enter the room, each with their own distinctive walk—Daire flashes in quickly, Astor saunters, and Valerian practically stomps. To be fair, he is a dragon, and they're not known for walking quietly. With nods to Fallon, they each claim a seat at the table.

"Thank you all for coming," I begin. "First, I want to bring you up to speed with current events." I detail the inconsistencies I've found in Arden's actions, the most recent display of her power, and her words in the elevator.

Daire frowns, then loudly protests, "I don't understand why we're getting more involved. The favor asked for employment, training, and research assistance. If she needs power or protection, let her get it from somebody else. Hell, she knows Lucifer. Let her ask him."

"What are you talking about?" I demand.

"Did you know she's a member of the House of Light and Karth?" Daire waits for my nod of agreement, then continues, "Karth is Vargas Karth, Lucifer's executioner. The one he calls upon when demons screw up. Not only is she considered family to Vargas, she also knows my father. Apparently, he has dinner over at their house regularly. So I'd say she already has friends— powerful friends."

Thinking about her being friends with Lucifer makes me want to smile. "That's one piece she hasn't hidden from us. I don't know why Vargas can't help her, but I know the Princess of the Light Fae wouldn't have formally asked for my favor if she'd had the ability to help Arden directly. The princess' political capital is limited. Many of the Fae didn't take it well when she mated with Lord Vargas. If she'd been anyone other than the princess and the queen's sister, she would've been shunned. What about Vargas?" I look at Daire for the answer.

"Maybe. I can ask my father," he grumbles reluctantly.

"Yes, please see what you can find out." My brain races as I think through the next steps. "I'll talk to the princess myself."

Astor leans forward. "I'm salivating at the thought of training her. Her power is immense. I've rarely encountered power of that magnitude, but to see it in a witch? Never. I've got a feeling she's a hybrid, like us. What do you think?"

"I agree. Based on the bits of information she's given, I think she knows more about her mother than she's told us. However, the favor asks us to assist her investigation into her history. I'm guessing she needs us to find her father," I deduce. "Her power feels like a witch. Could he be a witch, too? But she wouldn't be a hybrid, then. If she's a hybrid, then something powerful is preventing her from tapping into that side of herself."

"What can I do?" Valerian interjects.

"Glad you asked," I tell him with a smile and watch as he blanches. "Just kidding. She needs a sparring and weapons trainer. Someone good, she says. If she's been living with Vargas, I'm guessing she's going to give you a run for your money."

He leans back and crosses his arms, giving me a scowl. "You know how I feel about witches. They're fragile," he snarls. When he realizes I'm not backing down, he slams his palm on the table. "Fine, but I want the seventy-two-year-old bottle of Macallan in your office."

Now I'm scowling. "You want payment?" I sneer.

"Not payment for helping her. But payment for helping you? Abso-fucking-lutely," he growls. "Besides, I've been asking you for a wee sip of the Macallan for ages, and you won't open the bloody bottle. Since you won't share, you don't deserve it."

"Wait a minute, I want in on this action. After all, I'm

helping you, too," Astor interjects. "I want one hour with the dark Fae book of spells you have in your safe."

Fury rises. "How the hell do you know about that book?" I demand. I'd been purposely hiding it from him, knowing how the dark calls to him.

"I saw it when you took out the letter the other day. It was sitting there all shiny and precious. It called to me," he answers. "Is it a deal?"

"One hour," I reply, looking at Valerian and Daire. "I'll bring the bottle of Macallan to the training room tomorrow. Daire, what do you want?"

Daire stares at me and states, "I want the witch gone as soon as possible."

A small protest rises in me at his words, but I squelch them. "I agree," I reply.

Fallon, who's been watching the entire exchange, jumps in, "What do you need me to do?"

"I need you to investigate the assassination attempts. We'll see if Vargas or the princess have any more information, but if not, we need to get a handle on what or who we're facing here so we can prepare accordingly."

Fallon nods in agreement. "I'll put the word out to see if any of my father's assassins have heard of this contract. It'll be an easy enough place to start. I should finish with my mission in the next few days, and home to The Abbey by the end of the week."

Relief shows on all our faces at this news. We're all waiting for the day when he decides he's had enough of his father's machinations, but until then, we stand by and watch as these missions take their toll on him.

"Sounds good," I reply. "Let me know what this is going to cost me." Smirking, I hit end before he can reply.

"One day soon, you must tell us how the Princess of the Light Fae saved your life," Daire announces. "Maybe we could send her a fruit basket or something."

"Your sense of humor is dreadful. Honestly, I don't know the story. I only know my piece of it," I confess. "I'll ask Solandis if she can tell me how she came to know about the contract on my life and why she saved me." Another thing to add to our conversation.

"It took you long enough," the smooth, cultured voice on the phone admonishes me. "Did you think the life debt would be so easy to absolve?" The Princess of the Light Fae's laugh is as delicate and melodious as the female herself.

"My apologies, princess. I called with an update," I assert, slightly irritated with her reaction. I bring her up to speed with everything that's happened since Arden arrived, including the steps my cadre and I are taking next. "I'm calling you for any additional information about Arden and her situation you're willing to share. In addition, I'd also like to know the story of how you came to save my life."

"You ask for a lot," she remarks. "But for Arden, I'll do anything. She's a daughter to me, do you understand? Not by blood, but mine all the same. Her mother gave me guardianship of her when she was a few weeks old. She was a powerful seer and foresaw many things to come for Arden, for me, for herself, and even for you. She knew assassins were hunting Arden, so she gave her into my safekeeping, knowing she was forfeiting her own life in return. She couldn't tell me all of her visions, or risk Arden's destiny changing for the worse, but she gave me strict instructions to follow to keep Arden safe. And I followed them to the letter, until the day I had to send her away, to you. Her mother told me assassins would come for her in our home, and the Killian blade would appear to save her. Once this event occurred, she would need to leave us and find her destiny." She stops while I digest her words.

"Did I know her? Why would she send Arden to me?" I ask, trying to think of any seers I've met.

"She's the reason I saved you. You appeared in one of her visions, along with one of the Killian blades. The vision told her that saving you would be a tipping point in Arden's favor," she explains. "Vargas found out about the contract on your life, and we intervened at the exact moment she instructed."

"I see," I reply as a wave of gratitude toward Arden's mother sweeps over me. "Can you tell me the name of Arden's mother?"

"No, Arden will tell you when she's ready to trust you," she states.

"Can you tell me who ordered the contract?" I ask, wondering who would have access to one of the Killian blades. A chill runs up my spine at the thought of this particular blade.

A thousand years ago, an Elven blacksmith made three blades containing the power to kill a Fae. The blades, imbued with their own magic, randomly appear throughout history, both helping and hindering the destiny of the Fae.

The princess hesitates, then murmurs, "I didn't want to share this information with you, but you have a right to know. Your mother ordered the contract. We neutralized the threat to you by blackmailing her in return, but there will come a time when she feels the reward is worth the risk. Be careful. You're part of Arden's destiny. Without you, I fear for her."

She explains they don't have any leads on the assassination attempts. Vargas and Callyx have both turned the Underworld upside down to find clues, but none have surfaced. Maybe, with my access to other courts, I can find some new leads.

Reeling, I barely hear the end of the conversation. All I can think about is the fact that my mother tried to have me killed. My beautiful, icy dark Fae mother, who rarely even bothers herself with my affairs. What could she possibly gain?

8

ARDEN

A beast of a man waits for me in the training room. Arms crossed and stance wide, he takes up more space than any male I've ever encountered. He's massive, this King of Dragons and legendary warrior. Awe strikes me mute while I pause to capture him and this moment.

His aura screams lethal predator. Even Vargas is in awe of this warrior. Callyx, too, although he would deny it. And nothing I've ever heard about him is exaggerated. If anything, the tales don't do him justice.

I'm guessing he's six foot seven at a minimum, and like I said, a beast. My eyes travel from his enormous feet, encased in shit-kicking black boots, along the tree trunks he probably calls legs, to a barrel of a chest capped with massive shoulders.

Where does he even find clothes to fit? I eye the jeans and shirt he's wearing with skepticism.

His head swivels toward me, and he scowls.

I lock my jaw to prevent my mouth from dropping wide open. What they neglected to mention is how beautiful he is, but I guess it's not a surprise, as tales of warriors are told by men.

My eyes trace his strong, masculine features. Sharp cheekbones, cut high on his cheeks, sit above a jawline hewn from granite. His tousled jet-black hair and amber eyes are frosting on a decadent cake. And those lips...Even with a scowl, his full pouty lips beg to be nibbled.

Hesitantly, I stare at him, then remember my manners. "Hello, King Valerian." My voice breathless as I greet him, giving him a slight bow. "I'm Arden. It's a pleasure to meet you."

He glares at me and points to the track above us. "Five miles."

Rude. "Thank you, but I've already completed five miles today. In fact, I run five miles every morning. I'm ready to spar, if that works for you," I suggest sweetly. You catch more flies— or a grumpy king—with honey, right?

"I need to see what you're capable of doing, first. Then I'll tell you when we're ready to spar. Got it?" he snaps, pointing to the track again.

Biting my tongue, I head up to the track and finish five miles in record time, my anger driving me to sprint at full speed.

"Done," I call out with not even a hint of breathlessness. "What's next?"

His lips flatten when he glances at the stopwatch. "Tell me about your training up to this point," he demands.

"When I was a child, Vargas would bring in various masters to teach me different styles of fighting. I've accumulated brown or black belts in the various martial arts from Muay Thai to Krav Maga. Lately, I've been on a boxing kick, though. Nothing like punching a bag when frustrated, right?" I ask, grinning. Not an iota of response from him. Okay, then. "Vargas and I trained together almost every morning. If he was away, I'd train with Callyx, but he's tougher than Vargas."

He tilts his head to the side while he thinks through my words. "Well, I won't be easy on you like Vargas, but I'll try to be cognizant of your fragile human body," he states. "Who's Callyx, and why is training with him harder?"

I snort. As if Vargas would take it easy on anyone. Demon lords have little compassion or empathy. I don't argue. He'll see soon enough. "Callyx Karth is the son of Solandis and Vargas. He's also Lucifer's spy. Or assassin, depending on your point of view. Bastard uses unusual tactics, including a mix of shadows and illusion to fight."

A look of interest crosses his face. That's right. As the king of all dragons, he's mastered all of their powers, including fire, ice, and shadows. "He glamours the shadows?" Incredulity colors his tone.

"It's incredible. He can make shadows appear substantial. You don't even suspect it until you try to grab an imaginary weapon or punch an imaginary bad guy and meet air. There are slight tells, but in the heat of the fight, it's tough to recognize them," I explain, my excitement and frustration apparent. I can see his mind racing with thoughts on how to put this tactic to use with his own shadow dragons. With a Fae in their ranks, this would give them a serious advantage in battle.

He waves his hand, simultaneously dismissing the discussion and calling a staff to his hand. "Let's see what Vargas has taught you," he commands. "I'll take it easy on you until I'm sure you can defend yourself."

Using a push of magic, my personal staff, its weight and length customized for me, appears. My hands grip the smooth wooden pole, while my feet adjust to fighting stance.

For the first fifteen minutes, we test each other's skills,

attacking and defending, parrying and thrusting. The staccato of the staffs meeting in battle and an occasional grunt when one finds its mark are the only sounds in our silent battle.

Until he decides he's comfortable with my capabilities. Then he lets loose, and it's as if fucking Ares himself is raining down war on me. If I'd had any other trainer besides Vargas, I'd have been destroyed in the first minute. Thinking fast on my feet, I realize I need to use more than my physical strength.

Using spells, I enhance the staff until it's like a steel beam, each hit thunderous as it strikes his. Simultaneously, I pull up my battle shield and weave it around me, strengthening my protection from hits, spells, elemental powers, and whatever else he can dream up.

When I see a slight opening, my staff slips in and drops a lethal hit to his solar plexus. He grunts but doesn't move an inch. Damn dragon must be made of concrete.

For the first time since I entered the room, he smiles. Hells bells, he has a lot of teeth. Don't get me wrong, his smile is devastating, but the fact he's now smiling instead of scowling is worrisome. What the hell is he planning?

I don't have too long to wait. With a *whoosh*, he's holding a flaming staff and his grin is wider than ever. When a simple water spell doesn't work, I turn my staff to ice a millisecond before the two staffs meet, and a resounding hiss echoes in the room.

Calling up a glamour, I feint, making it look as if I'm lowering my staff to swipe at his feet, but instead, I shift to the side to catch the back of his knees. Before I'm even in position, he jumps and spins towards me. The tip of his staff catches my chest, and it's as if he used Thor's hammer to hit me. I fly backwards into the far wall, then slide down to the base, plaster raining down on me like snow.

"Fuck, Valerian! I asked you to train her, not kill her," Lord

Theron shouts from the far side of the room. His shouting betrays his concern like nothing else. It's nice to see a crack in his lordship's icy veneer.

The training floor shakes as Valerian runs over to me. As he bends over to check my pulse, I leap up and catch his chin with my staff. A power spell ensures the hit is hard enough to knock this dragon on his ass, and it works, laying him out for a couple of seconds. I use the precious time to leap up and get into a fighting stance.

Raising his head off the floor, he glares at me for a second before roaring with laughter. "Well played, lass," he says, still chuckling. He extends his hand for me to help him up, but I shake my head. I stopped falling for that trick when I was three.

With a flip, he's up and charging at me. You wouldn't think a big guy like him could be so fast, but he's like a damn jet plane.

Bringing my staff up, I turn his staff into flowers before it slams into mine. He changes the flowers into shards of ice. The deadly spears sing through the air as they head towards me. With wind, I redirect the ice towards the wall on my left, and they thud into the wall, one after another.

With his staff gone, he could easily conjure up another weapon but decides to use his bare hands. I scoff. A man might feel obligated to drop his weapons to give him a fair fight, but I don't. I need every advantage I can get.

Damn, his arm's reach is long. Countering an attack on one side, I quickly realize I need to be in two places at once. With a whisper, my staff splits into two, and I use them to parry his next punch, my staffs against his fists.

Faster and faster we fight, both of us in our zones. I hear the door opening in the far corner, but I don't dare take my eyes off Valerian. Damn sneaky devil. A long claw extended from his hand a second ago and sheared off a tip of my staff. We dance around the room, neither of us giving an inch. It's not an equal match, by any means. I've got a feeling he's holding back, but at least I'm giving him a fight worthy of his time.

A blur appears in my peripheral, and without thinking, I turn and strike. Just as I hit, a claw reaches out and flays open my back. A short scream escapes me. I fall to my knees for a brief second, then leap up into a fighting stance a few feet away. The wound burns and drops trickle down my back. Confusion clouds my mind. What the hell?

"Daire, what the fuck?" Valerian roars. He puts out a hand towards me in a gesture of peace. "It's okay. It's only Daire. Let me see your back, lass. I think I got you pretty good."

Daire stands there stunned for a second. "It's as if you knew I was there, but it's impossible. Did you feel the air move?"

With a shrug, I lower my weapons. "I saw a blur to the side, and in the heat of the battle, I failed to think and struck out. Dammit, Vargas would be so fucking disappointed I left my rear exposed," I lament, groaning at my stupidity.

"Disappointed?" Daire studies my face. "You hit a vampire, and not any vampire, but me. I'd say it's pretty incredible. Most humans can't see us."

"I-I'm…" I stutter, trying to figure out how to tell them.

"Lass!" Valerian shouts to get my attention. "Turn around so I can see your back!"

"Do you need to shout?" a cool voice intervenes. "We have guests." Stepping back, Lord Theron reveals the witches. "Now, what have you done to her back?"

Shit. I step closer to Valerian in an attempt to disguise my power as his. I can't fight Valerian without having access to my full power, but I don't want the witches to know how powerful I am yet. "Nothing. He thought he scratched me, but as you can see, I'm fine," I assert, turning around to show them my back. My shirt, entirely whole, drapes from my back with not a drop of blood anywhere. "If you give me a second to use the restroom and clean up, I'll be right with you. I think you mentioned we were testing bloodline one today?" Seeing their nod, I grab Valerian's hand and step out into the hallway.

"Where's the restroom?" I ask, wiping the sweat from my face.

He tugs on my hand. "Lass, drop the glamour and let me see your back," he demands.

Sighing, I drop the glamour. He steps closer, and I inhale, catching the smell of a bonfire on a crisp winter evening and sweat. Turning my back to him, I wince as he pulls pieces of my shirt away from the wound. Although it's already healing, the initial cut was pretty deep and it's still tender. I bite my lip, waiting for his questions.

Blunt-tipped fingers caress the area around the wound. "I'm so sorry, lass." His voice gruff with relief. "But how can you already be healing? Do you have a healing spell woven into your shield? Or did you take a healing potion?"

"I never thought of weaving a healing spell into my shield, but it's a great idea," I muse, turning to peer up at him. Worry creases his brow, and it's all I can do to stop myself from reaching out and smoothing it away.

Making sure nobody is around, I pull his head down and whisper in his ear, "It's not a healing spell or potion. It's natural. I'm immortal." Releasing his neck, I stare up at him, waiting for my words to filter into his brain.

He's stunned for a second before relief flashes in his eyes. He props an arm against the wall and leans down to whisper back, "We're definitely going to have a chat about this later." With a tilt of his head, he indicates now is not the time with the witches here.

Suddenly, a broad grin splits his face. "Well, lass, guess we can have us a real battle next time," he declares, walking off with a whistle.

A real battle? I knew the damn dragon was holding back.

I'm more relieved than angry he took the news so well. I wonder if he'll tell the others or if I should. Glancing back at the training room, I realize I'll have to figure it out later. I don't want the witches here any longer than necessary. Spooling in my power and cleaning myself up, I step back into the training room.

9

VALERIAN

Daire joins me as I stride away from Arden. Silently communicating with him, I continue to whistle until we're out of hearing range. Relief slams into me. My knees give out, and I stop and lean against the wall.

Immortal! Thank fuck, she's immortal, I scream silently.

"Are you okay?" Daire enquires softly, his eyes assessing my reaction.

Joy spears through me. "She's not hurt. In fact, she's healing rapidly," I assure him.

He stiffens. "I didn't ask about her. I asked if you were okay," he says, frowning. "But I guess it's good to know she isn't hurt. We don't need the Princess of the Light Fae and Vargas Karth breathing down our necks." He shrugs, her health of little importance to him.

"She's not healing from a spell or a potion. Her immortality is healing her," I explain to him with a huge grin. "I don't have to worry about my carelessness causing the death of another witch."

Shocked, Daire doesn't move a muscle as he processes my words. "That's why she can see me, and how she could defend herself against you," he intones, his mind going back to the training room. "If she'd have told us about her immortality in the beginning, I'd have known not to stand so damn close." He shudders as if he felt the scrape of my claw across her back. I guess he might care more than he protests.

With a slap on my back, Daire jokes, "Theron looked ready to murder you. Guess you'll live another day." His grin becomes evil. "I can't wait to see the look on his face when he realizes she's immortal. Guess Astor was right, the bastard. She's a hybrid. I can't wait to find out what she's made of." This time, he's whistling as he walks away. It sounds like "The Devil Went Down to Georgia" by Charlie Daniels.

Daire's telling jokes, Theron's emotions are slipping, and Astor's protecting her against handsy wolves. And me, sparring with a witch. I shake my head as I turn towards my room. The last time my life changed this much, the people I loved the most were killed. One by me.

As I enter my room, the top drawer calls to me like a beacon. Forcing my steps over to it, I pull it open and take out a small portrait. Moira stares back at me, a quirk to her eyebrow indicating her mischievous nature, and the small smile she displayed only for me on her face. My fingers trace her features, while my mind slips into the past.

Moira MacAllister gave me this portrait as a declaration, to one and all, of her love for me. If I'd known it would be the catalyst for her death and the darkest days of my life, I'd have destroyed it immediately. Instead, I treasured it, a simple thing that meant her love was real, not just a tumble in the hay between a witch and a dragon. I didn't know its very existence would drive my father into a rage and cause both their deaths. And the birth of my reign.

I put the portrait and memories back in the drawer before walking over to my desk. *Work waits for no man, or king*, I muse, picking up the phone to make some calls.

DAIRE IS STANDING AT THE RAILING, ALONE FOR A CHANGE, WHEN I walk up and slap him on the back. "How are things going this evening?" I ask, my eyes scanning the dance floor and tables.

He shrugs and responds dryly, "The same as it's been for a few millennia. They come, they play, sometimes they come and play, but besides the décor, it's the same."

"Not everything," I murmur, my eyes tracking Arden as she waits tables. "She's shaking things up, changing us, and she just arrived. What's it going to be like in a few months?"

"Speak for yourself," he retorts. Smoothing down his shirt, he flicks an imaginary piece of lint off the silk button-down. "I haven't changed at all."

I snort, then tease him, "No? Why were you in the training room today? And you're standing here alone on a Saturday night. Where's Solange?"

"Simple curiosity. And Solange is having a girls' night," he replies, pointing to his girlfriend, who's sitting at a table below us. She glances up and blows him a kiss, and he nods at her in return.

The lights flicker, indicating a performance. My face betrays little emotion as I turn towards the stage. I rarely watch the races battle, but I'm already standing here and to leave would be an insult, even if the dragons are not performing.

They don't come here often, only when forced to pay homage to their king, and they always give me notice. It's a mockery, but it's been this way for a thousand years, and I don't see it changing soon. A brief feeling of regret resonates through me before I chase it away.

Focusing on the stage, I watch five light witches dressed in cowboy boots, plaid shirts, and tiny ass jean shorts strut onto the dance floor. *Fuck*, it's the monthly battle of the witches—light versus dark. It doesn't help when the two witches leading the battle are bitter rivals.

The dark witches line up on the edge of the stage to watch their competitors perform. Arden, unknowingly, steps up beside them. One of them elbows the dark witch leader and dips her chin towards Arden. I tense.

The music starts, drawing the crowd's attention. Cages drop from the ceiling, the light witches step in them, and they rise about ten feet in the air. With a spell, the dance floor turns into a pit of fire. The crowd roars, knowing they're going to get a show.

A few bars from a piano sound, announcing "Raising Hell" by Kesha. While the crowd isn't a fan of witches, they know better than to offend them. And of course, the males greatly appreciate every suggestive dance move and boot stomp the beautiful witches make. Whistles pierce the air when they rip off their plaid shirts, revealing black bras underneath. With the last bars of the song ringing in the air, they drop to their knees, hold their hands up in prayer, and bow their heads until the song ends. The crowd cheers wildly.

With their plaid shirts back on, they douse the fire and lower the cages. After stepping out, they link hands and bow to the crowd, then head straight towards Arden.

I tense. My glance at Daire has him using his vampiric hearing to listen to their conversation.

"My aunt says you're doing well with the testing. Not as well as me, of course," Cassandra says flippantly, "but if you can affiliate yourself with four bloodlines like you say you can, you'll probably be able to hang out with us." She sweeps her arm to indicate the rest of the witches with her.

With a glance over her shoulder at the dark witches, she warns Arden, "Make sure you don't make the wrong decision when you join the coven, or you'll end up with losers. Oh, my mother is sending you an invitation to meet the council tomorrow night. Make sure you dress appropriately." A toss of her hair, and the witch leaves the dance floor with the others in tow.

"An invitation to the council? What are they up to now?" I murmur to Theron, who's stepped up to join us.

"I don't know, but she won't be going alone," he assures me. We both turn back to watch Arden below.

Arden frowns at Cassandra, then glances over to the dark witches, who are now glaring at her. It's easy to see from this angle that the bitch Cassandra accomplished her goal. The dark witches think Arden's aligning herself with Cassandra.

A gong sounds, and the dark witches shift their attention toward the stage. With a whisper of magic, their outfits change from casual to costume in a blink of an eye. Black thigh highs and matching knee-high heeled boots are paired with a black bustier and a microscopic black leather miniskirt.

"The clothes get tinier and tinier as the years go by," Theron remarks dryly.

Daire grins. "I sure as hell don't mind," he retorts with a lick of his lips, as if the lack of clothing is an open invitation to biting wherever he pleases.

Theron shakes his head in disappointment. "No class," he states.

"Just because their outfits are skimpy doesn't mean they lack class," he chides Theron.

"He meant you," I roar, laughing at him.

A low growl escapes when he turns to Theron. "I'm a prince. You're a lowly lord. What do you know about class?"

"I assure you..." Before Theron can finish the sentence, the dark witch performance begins. This time, a violin plays the opening bars of "Salt" by Ava Max. Unlike the light witches, this performance isn't for the crowd. Oh, they're entertained, but it's more for the personal message it's sending than the performance. The dark witches dance hard and their voices ring out, but their attention remains on a solitary figure at the back of the crowd.

A few jeers and a slap on the back of an incubus identifies their intended target. It's the same incubus who led the performance Astor favored the other night.

Salt appears on the dance floor, and the witches slide through it, picking it up in their hands and flinging it up in the air as they dance until it covers everyone. A few crystals land on my sleeve, and I brush them off, scowling at the dance floor. The performances irritate me, but it beats breaking up fights every night.

The song ends, and the leading dark witch hands Arden a card as she walks past her. Going straight up to the incubus, she flings salt directly at him, then stalks off in the opposite direction, her trail of minions behind her.

We all know salt keeps a demon out of your house, and the crowd roars with laughter at the intended message. At least this performance was interesting. As I look over at Arden, she's staring down at the card in her hands with a pensive expression on her face. I wonder what it says.

10

ARDEN

M y spine tingles, alerting me to a supernatural presence, right before an envelope slips under my hotel door. Witchfire flares in my hand, ready to fire in my defense. With my magic, I slowly open the door, but find the hallway empty.

With a wave, the door closes, and I pick up the envelope and open it to find tonight's invite. I stand there staring at the black card with my name embossed in gold. Butterflies erupt inside me at this momentous event, and my fingers trace over my name repeatedly, my witch heritage literally at my fingertips. Tonight is a simple meeting with key members of the coven, but it's momentous because it's the first step in finding out why my mother wanted me to hide from the witches.

Hmm...It doesn't say to come alone, I reflect. I tap the card against my palm.

Picking up my phone, I send a text to two very different

people. Now that's done, I need to find something *appropriate* to wear.

———————

WHEN I FEEL THE TINGLES THIS TIME, I OPEN THE DOOR WITHOUT waiting for the knock. "Good evening, Lord Theron," I murmur in greeting. "If you wouldn't mind coming in for a second, I need your help."

He stands in the doorway, impeccably dressed in a navy suit and purple tie, which enhances his violet eyes further and matches my form-fitting deep purple dress. "Good evening," he says tersely, the air snapping with cold around him.

I guess someone's in a snit, I muse.

With a wave, I gesture for him to enter. As he passes, a waft of his delicious scent of winter and dark chocolate follows, and my nipples peak at the intoxicating smell. I close my eyes, savoring the feeling for a brief second, then focus on the reason I invited him into my room.

"Would you mind zipping me up?" I plead, turning my back to him. I hear a harsh exhale, a pause, and the anger snapping at the edges of his composure mellows. Cool fingers trace down my spine before capturing the zipper and pulling it up.

With a shiver, I turn to face him, but he hasn't moved. A couple of inches separate us, and with my heels on, there's little difference in our height, making my mouth line up perfectly with his, my glossy lips millimeters from his firm ones. Barely breathing, I fight the urge to close the distance.

My eyes meet his. Desire flares between us, and the air turns heavy with need. My heart pounds as I wait for his next move. His violet eyes sweep down to my lips, which I lick, and he sucks in a breath. My hands reach out to pull him to me but find nothing but air.

I blink, bringing the room back into focus. He's now standing by the door, holding it open. "If we don't leave now, we'll be late," he says, completely ignoring the moment.

With a toss of my hair, I bend over to smooth my stockings. When I hear him mutter, I smile and stand up.

He's not as indifferent as he likes to pretend, I think, relieved my desire is not one-sided.

As I turn towards the door, I sweep up the invitation and my clutch. "I'm sure you'll get us there on time," I jibe softly, knowing he would never let us be late. It goes against every fiber of his being.

A MATTE BLACK MASERATI SITS IN THE HOTEL CARPORT WAITING for us. I snort. The Fae love luxury and fast cars. Even in the land of the Fae, they drive cars from this dimension, although they power them with magic instead of gasoline. I sink down into the seat, and it hugs me, wrapping me in the smell of leather and…him.

As he starts the car, I turn to him. "How long does it take to get there?"

"Twenty-two minutes," he answers, glancing down at my legs. My dress has pulled up from when I sat down, and at almost six feet tall, there's a lot of leg on display.

"That's precise," I remark. Wiggling, I pull down my dress an inch or two. I don't want him too distracted.

The car eases out of the hotel drive, making brief turns until we hit the interstate, where he floors it. I can't even register how fast we're going. It's a deliberate message, and I can't help but laugh at its delivery.

"I guess Valerian told you I was immortal?" I drawl, guessing at his anger.

"He did," he replies curtly. "Why didn't you tell me?"

"You didn't ask," I state. "I'm three hundred and twenty-eight years old. How old are you? And the others?"

"You didn't want me to ask. You wanted me to think of you as a human witch with moderate powers, who needed assistance finding your heritage," he seethed.

Ah, he's putting together a few pieces. No wonder he's pissed.

"You're right," I concede.

He whips around to stare at me.

"Watch the road," I yell as we veer off it. "I might not die easily, but it would sure as hell hurt. I wanted you to see me in that light, but I didn't lie to you."

Scoffing, he easily brings the car back in line. "You might not have lied, but you deceived me just the same."

"Semantics. In a hurry to get rid of the life debt hanging over your shoulders, you brushed aside your instincts and leapt at the opportunity. If you had asked questions, I'd have answered." I cross my arms and glare at him.

"Right," he sneers.

"Solandis told me not to lie to you. I would have spoken truthfully," I admit. She warned me it would piss him off, but too much was riding on the decision. I couldn't take the chance he wouldn't help me.

"I spoke to Solandis the other night," he tells me. "She said you would give me more information when you trusted me. Is that correct?" He stares at me, searching for the truth instead of waiting for the words. "We'll table this for now." He points to a vast mansion on the hill. "The coven's house is called Witchwood, and it's served as the headquarters of the witches' council and their ceremonial place for hundreds of years."

Eyeing the structure, I realize the witches are quite wealthy. The mansion is hundreds of years old, maybe more. The house stretches for acres and comprises of architecture from different eras. Columns, towers, corbels, arches, and more are thrown together haphazardly but with a certain flair. The entire structure is cream, which seems to both unify the house and subdue the chaos.

Pulling up to the front door, I wait as a man in a black uniform opens my car door. "Thank you, sir," I tell him quietly, nerves suddenly attacking me. I've waited for this moment for a very long time, and I don't know what I'll find.

"My pleasure, miss. Please, call me Henry. I'm the butler here at Witchwood," he responds stiffly, as if unused to being thanked. He holds out his arm to escort me, but I look around for Lord Theron.

"I'm her escort," he pronounces coolly, his arm raised for me to take, his usual stoic demeanor intact.

"My pardon, sir. I wasn't told to expect anyone else," he explains.

"We didn't invite anyone else," a striking voice rings out. "You're dismissed, Henry."

Henry gives me a sly wink and a slight bow. "Nice to meet you, miss. Sir." He walks up the steps and past the woman standing there, waiting impatiently for me to acknowledge her.

"Good evening, I'm Arden and this is Lord Theron," I state confidently as I introduce us.

Beauty, power, and elegance are weaved into this woman's bones. Standing straight and tall in an elegant black cocktail dress, her dark brown hair contained in a sleek chignon, she flashes dark brown eyes at Lord Theron, then turns to me. "Hello, Arden. Nice to meet you. I'm Caro Pennington, leader of the coven and our council. Please come in," she responds airily, before continuing. "We didn't expect you to bring someone, especially an aristocratic Fae, to our little gathering. We would have prepared a more sumptuous celebration if we'd known." She chides me as if I'm a child. I guess she thinks me the same age as her daughter, Cassandra.

"Oh, please forgive me. I should have mentioned Lord Theron is currently my de facto guardian," I say smoothly, as if

I'm not dropping a bomb on her. "And since I didn't have transportation to get here, I asked if he wouldn't mind driving me. Thankfully, he agreed. Isn't he wonderful?" There seems to be no love lost between these two. I laugh silently and wink up at him.

Surprisingly, a super tiny smirk appears and his eyes dance with glee. "I'd never let her enter a stranger's house while under my protection," he confirms, adding his own polite warning to Caro. "Is there a problem with my attendance?"

"We don't allow outsiders to join our celebrations," she sputters.

"Oh, I thought this was a simple meet and greet. I didn't realize it was a celebration. I'd have worn something more *appropriate*." I deliberately use the same word Cassandra used to instruct me on my attire. Her eyes glance at my form fitting couture dress, and her mouth tightens.

"I'll make an exception this one time," she warns. "Come along, everyone's waiting for you." She strides off, heels clicking against the marble floor.

I squeeze Theron's arm, thanking him for his protection. He didn't have to put himself between her and I, but he did, and for that, I'm grateful. I owe him an apology and some answers. At least, the few I know.

Entering the room, I stop and gaze at the witches in attendance. Most of them are strangers, but a few known faces stand out. Bianca waves at me from the corner. Cassandra stands with her usual posse in the center of the room. Clare hovers in the doorway, only stepping back as we arrive.

Caro sweeps out her arm. "Welcome to Witchwood. We can't officially welcome you to the coven until after your placement ceremony, but you can meet the most important witches tonight."

"Why thank you, Caro," a deep voice resonates behind me, and I turn around. "We misplaced our invitation, but we're thrilled to be here to meet Arden. She should meet all the leaders, correct?"

His arm circles the young woman stepping up beside him. Two additional women flank them both. He raises an eyebrow towards me, then asks, "Have we started the introductions?"

Caro gives me a suspicious look before greeting the newcomers. "Hello, Santiago, Amelie, and Katrina. And you, too, of course, Reyna." She greets the young woman last, and I'm guessing it's how they rank in importance to her. "We're just getting to the introductions. Allow me."

He nods his head, indicating for her to go ahead, and her mouth tightens at his arrogance. The tension between the original group and this one is palpable.

Pursing her lips, she walks around the room. "As you know, I'm Caro, leader of the coven and witches' council. I'm also leader of bloodline three. I'll introduce each of the council members, then I'll leave you to introduce yourself to the others."

I nod in agreement, my mind automatically filling in the blanks. Bloodline three known for their mastery of spell casting and shielding.

Stepping to her left, she puts her hand on a handsome black-haired man. "This is Adam Pennington, my husband and leader of bloodline four."

I shake his hand. "It's nice to meet you, Adam." His handshake is weak, barely grazing my fingertips. Never trust a man with a weak handshake, Vargas always told me. Weak handshakes equal weak character. Adam is bloodline four, which is mastery of healing and potions, one of the talents I haven't tested for yet.

Caro walks over to a handsome dark-complected man, trailing her hand over his bicep. She squeezes it, then turns him towards me. "This is Nico Perrone, leader of bloodline one."

He winks at me before pronouncing in a heavy Italian accent, "It's a pleasure to meet such a beautiful woman, Arden." He picks up my hand and places a wet kiss on it.

A cool wind brushes over my hand, drying it, then Lord Theron's thumb brushes across the spot, rubbing away the sloppy kiss. Murmuring a soft thank you, I tuck my hand into the crook of his arm.

Nico Perrone. I'm not sure if I'm more startled by him or the fact he's leader of bloodline one. I thought Bianca was the leader. Looking at her, I see her smiling at Nico with love. "Hello, it's nice to meet you. I apologize for staring. I thought Bianca was leader of bloodline one. My mistake."

"My sister has moderate power," he explains, shrugging. "She could never lead our family."

From the corner of my eye, I see Bianca dip her head to the floor, and I frown at this show of submission. "Well, she's been wonderful to me. Very welcoming," I enthuse. Her head pops up, and she smiles.

"That's good," he tells me, tossing a smile over his shoulder to Bianca.

Caro gestures to the man still standing in the doorway. He's good-looking, around forty-five years old, with dark brown hair and golden eyes. "Santiago Martinez, leader of bloodline six, and his daughter, Reyna." Bloodline six, transfiguration.

"It's truly a pleasure to welcome you to our coven, Arden. My daughter Reyna is about your age, and she would be happy to help you get acclimated," he says smoothly, drawing his daughter forward. His eyes gleam with opportunity.

"I'm so glad you could make it, both of you," I drawl, subtly thanking them for attending without informing Caro of the invitation I extended to them both. Given Cassandra's underhanded introduction to the dark witches the other night, I could only guess how it would have looked later when they found out they missed my original introduction to the coven.

Reyna gives me a cool greeting. "It's nice to meet you."

Before Caro can introduce the next council leader, the tall

redhead reaches out and grabs my hand, introducing herself. "I'm Katarina Ivanov, leader of bloodline five."

Bloodline five, mastery of elemental powers. I smile at Katarina in return.

A curt voice pipes in with the remaining introduction. "I'm Amelie Von Dietrich, leader of bloodline two."

The tiny blonde woman gives me a nod but doesn't step forward to shake my hand. Interesting. Bloodline two, mastery of illusion and glamour. I glance at Theron and find him assessing Amelie, too. I wonder why she's wearing such a heavy glamour?

Caro interjects, "And this is Cassandra, my daughter, the most powerful witch in our coven. She's affiliated with five bloodlines. I believe you've met her friends? And of course, this is my other daughter, Charlotte."

Cassandra crosses her arms. "Of course we've met, Mother. We should go shopping later this week, okay?" Her eyes didn't miss my appropriate attire, and I know she's wondering if I can afford it or if it's borrowed.

"That would be lovely," I reply with a smile.

Caro looks happy with this latest plan. "Now that you've met everyone, let's sit down, shall we?" She directs Lord Theron and I over to the couch. Everyone else drifts over and finds a spot somewhere close to us.

Once we're comfortable with something to drink and appetizers nearby, she launches into the real reason behind tonight's invite. "We usually like to invite a new witch and their parents to our meet and greets. Tell me, dear, where are your parents?"

"My mother is dead, and I don't know my father's location," I reply. "My guardians raised me."

"Do you know your mother's name?" Her voice is sharp as she digs deeper.

"I'm sure that information is written somewhere," I vaguely answer. "I'll ask my guardian."

"Why don't you tell us about your guardians?" she asks, her voice high with forced enthusiasm.

My smile is genuine as I describe my family. "My guardians are wonderful, and I'm lucky they agreed to adopt me." I pause, before continuing, "My adopted mother is Fae. She and V—her mate raised me as if I were their own child. Even when they had their own child, I never felt as if I didn't belong. Anything I needed, they provided, including training. They invited tutors from everywhere to visit us, but given our isolated existence, I only met a few witches growing up. Thankfully, they could teach me the basics, but they weren't inclined to share their witch knowledge, which made it tough to trace my roots."

Caro blanches. "Fae?" Her eyes dart to Lord Theron before continuing. "Interesting. That's probably why the witches with-held their knowledge. We only like to share our heritage with other witches. I'm sure the Fae are protective of their secrets, as well."

"Of course," I assure her, even though I want to scream at her for her obvious disregard for the Fae. Lord Theron subtly squeezes my arm, and I glance down at my hands to regain my composure.

She continues her interrogation. "You don't remember the names of the witches that tutored you, do you? And tell me about your home. Where did you live that was so isolated?"

Tilting my head to the side, I try to look as if I'm thinking about it. "Sorry, I remember little about the witches because I was pretty young. One was a woman, with brown eyes and red hair. I want to say her name was Anna, but I'm not positive. The other witch was a man with brown eyes and hair, and his name was Tom or Thomas." I shrug and smile. "We lived on the edge of the Wilds. Are you familiar with that area?"

Her eyes widen. "The Wilds? I didn't realize anyone actually lived there. Wasn't that dangerous?" Her lip curls as if she's discovered a bug in her food.

"Yes it was, but we learned to be careful. Fortunately, most of the inhabitants nearby kept to themselves," I explain.

The crowd around us stirs, murmuring to each other. The Wilds is a dangerous and alien place to these individuals. With their immaculate houses and intimate knowledge of each other, they can't imagine living in an unknown environment, far from the rest of the coven.

Caro's frustration at the lack of information is abundantly clear. "Do you have a grimoire? It's a large book of spells that's typically passed from witch to witch. The ancestry of the book is written within it."

Interesting. My grimoire didn't have any names in it. "Really? I don't recall seeing any names in mine. But I have one."

Her eyes light up. "That's wonderful. Why don't you bring it by here, and we'll go through it together?" Relieved to have discovered a lead, she doesn't wait for my response, but stands and glances at Clare. "We will find your family, dear. Then we can be sure your placement ceremony is the best it can be. Now, why don't I give you a quick tour of Witchwood? Shall we?" She strides over to the doorway with only a quick glance back to see if we're following.

Lord Theron stands and helps me up. "That sounds lovely," I tell her.

11

ARDEN

Witchwood is impressive. We tour the council's chambers, where they create witch policy and law, and the adjoining room, where they hear cases and disputes.

Caro shows off the grand ballroom, glittering with magic and sparkling with gems. If I hadn't been to the light Fae court, the display of wealth would be staggering. It's still impressive, though.

She seems to care a lot about their wealth. In every room, Caro touts the expense of the furnishings and upkeep it takes to keep it thriving.

"What's our source of revenue? Who decides the best way to spend it? Is there a budget the coven reviews to make sure it's spent according to plan?" I question her.

Her mouth tightens. "When you're part of the coven, we'll discuss all the important details, dear. Don't forget, you brought an outsider to our meet and greet today," she reminds me curtly.

Raising an eyebrow, I stare at her, then give her my best smile. "Of course, how silly of me. I look forward to our discussion later."

"I'm so glad you understand. We appreciate you coming out and meeting us, and we're looking forward to the placement ceremony. You should finish the testing in the next week or two, right?" She waits for me to nod. We approach the front door, and Henry silently appears in time to open it for us. "Well, you've seen most everything. Unfortunately, it's late and the others have already left, but you can visit with them once you're a member. Cassandra will be in touch for your little shopping trip. Bring your grimoire over soon. It's important to understand your lineage before the placement ceremony. Have a good evening."

With those words, she turns on her heels and leaves us with Henry. "The car is ready for you in the driveway, sir. Have a good evening," he tells us.

I can barely contain my laughter as I glance at Lord Theron.

I guess they're kicking us out.

Apparently, bringing a Fae lord to the witch meet and greet was a big no-no. I stroll out the door. "Ta-ta, Henry, I'll see you soon," I call out, waving my fingers at him.

Lord Theron helps me into the car. As soon as he looks at me, I bust out laughing.

"An enlightening evening. I'm guessing you knew my attendance would play havoc with Caro's agenda?" he muses while pushing the button to start the car.

I did. And yet, I hadn't expected him to tell Caro I was under his protection, to draw a line in the sand. I mentally trace each of his perfectly symmetrical features, wondering why he is so willing to help me. "It's time I brought you up to speed with what I know," I tell him, my face serious. "And I apologize for my deception. Coming to you was not my choice, but letting you believe the task would be simple was my decision. I didn't know if I could trust you, and with my life and others at stake, I needed to be sure. If you hear my story and feel it's too much, I can ask Solandis to consider your life debt paid in full."

He stares intently for a minute, reading my face. When convinced of my sincerity, he puts the car in drive and takes off. "Tell me," he demands.

"I guess the best place to start would be the beginning. My mother was Gia Perrone, the second most powerful witch seer in history." I pause, breathless for a few seconds. I've never said those words to anyone. Solandis knew my mother but forbid me to tell anyone.

"Before I was born, Solandis and my mother met at a Fae ball. In fact, my mother specifically attended to meet Solandis. She'd seen the Princess of the Light Fae's mate in a vision and felt compelled to tell her. Solandis didn't believe her, especially since my mother saw a demon lord in her future and not the Fae Solandis loved at the time. But when Solandis met her mate, Vargas, she realized my mother's vision was accurate. They became fast friends."

Lord Theron pulls into an overlook and parks. When the car lights go off, the night sky surrounds us, sparkling and clear, while the city shines in the distance. "I always wondered how the Princess of the Light Fae could love a demon lord. I didn't realize they were mates," he remarks quietly. He turns towards me, closing the distance between us in the car.

"Mmm...and they're so in love, it's disgusting and beautiful," I confirm with a laugh, before continuing my story. "Solandis and my mother stayed in touch over the years. One night, my mother appeared on Solandis' doorstep, pregnant and alone, asking for her help. She needed somewhere safe to hide, where she could have her baby. They created a pocket dimension around Solandis' home, moved it to the edge of the Wilds, and hid from the world. My mother lived there with Solandis and Vargas until she had me." I tell the story as Solandis told it to me, but I can't help but imagine being pregnant and fearing for the safety of my child.

"After I was born, my mother's visions became more frequent. She wrote some of them down for Solandis, but others she kept to herself, for fear of influencing the future and my destiny too much. For the next few weeks, she gave Solandis many instructions. The biggest one? I must live in the bubble they created. While I could visit the land of the Fae or the Underworld, I was to avoid the human world and witches until the third Killian blade appeared." My voice is tight as I explain, the years of isolation having taken their toll. I look at him. "She even instructed Solandis to save your life."

He stares out into the night, a contemplative expression on his face. "Solandis told me your mother was the reason she and Vargas stepped in to save my life."

I nod. "When the second Killian blade appeared to Solandis, it was a sign. She said it appeared the night you met?" I ask, waiting for him to confirm.

"The assassin who came for me had a Killian blade," he admits. "I'd met Solandis earlier that evening."

Nodding, I continue, "In my mother's visions, the Killian blades appear three times. Each time, they serve as a signal for Solandis to follow the corresponding instructions my mother gave to her. When she saved your life, it was the second time a Killian blade appeared. Right before I arrived here, assassins entered our home and the third Killian blade made its appearance. I left and came to you the next day."

He taps his fingers lightly on my arm while he thinks, and I smile. He probably doesn't even realize he's doing it.

"What about the first time the blade appeared?" he asks, shifting the attention back to the story.

"According to Solandis, my mother left their home to find my father. She hadn't heard from him in a few months, but they'd set up a time and place to meet in case anything happened. We don't know what happened when she got there, but a few days later, Solandis found her dead, the first Killian blade buried in her chest," I say, my voice hoarse as I explain.

He seems puzzled. "A Killian blade is overkill for a human witch. And your father?"

"He wasn't there. I don't know who my father is, where he lives, or anything about him," I explain sadly and continue, "my mother never told Solandis much about my father, except he was an immortal and if his family found me, they'd kill me. To prevent me from finding my father before it was time, she bound the powers I inherited from him. Once I claim my witch heritage, the binding is supposed to fade and give me a clue to my other half."

"I'm sorry to hear about your mom," he says sincerely.

"Thank you. It's strange, though. My mother gave birth to me, obviously loved me very much, even sacrificed her life to keep me safe. And I'm grateful. But the best gift she gave me was Solandis. I don't feel like I ever missed having a mother," I explain, and my voice cracks slightly. I miss Solandis. This is the first time I've ever been away from her.

"That's understandable. Tonight must have felt strange, walking into an unfamiliar heritage. You've always known you were a witch, right?" He waits for my nod, then continues, "You know your mother's last name. Why didn't you tell them?"

"My mother forced Solandis to hide me from the witches. She brought in a couple of tutors, but they never knew my name. Why?" I muse. "Until I've figured out the reason, I'm keeping them in the dark. It's weird and sad. I felt so isolated from everyone growing up, especially when we would visit the Fae and I saw their sense of community and belonging. A coven is something I dreamed of my entire life. A place where I could learn and make friends with others like me. But I felt nothing tonight. Honestly, after meeting Caro and the others, I'm glad I haven't given them any information. The air in Witchwood is heavy with layers of intrigue and undercurrents. The coven feels like a one woman show, where Caro seems to have all the power and the others serve as props for her agenda instead of the coven's benefit. Instead of this grand world, it felt small and petty."

He hesitatingly explains, "You're unlike most witches I've met. They seem to have a superiority complex which exceeds most of their talents. And yet, their numbers are dwindling. About a thousand years ago, with the exception of the demons and Fae, witches outnumbered most supernatural races. They used their power to gain riches and wealth, sometimes at the expense of others, and many races feared them. Unfortunately, their exclusivity became their downfall. The bloodlines became diluted, with fewer witches born every year. They must be salivating at finding a new witch. I'm sure it's why they wanted to test you right away. Maybe you can add new powers to the coven." He pauses in thought. "It might also be the reason behind the assassination attempts."

"Maybe? I don't know. Merindah gave me a book on witch heritage. I'm about halfway through it, but I've spotted nothing unusual. Of course, I don't know enough about witches to spot anything irregular yet, but it's an interesting book. Caro's family is one of the original founding families. No wonder she's so smug...and powerful," I concede.

"Your power exceeds hers considerably, but I recommend keeping that fact hidden for a while. Caro is power hungry, and who knows what tricks she has up her sleeve. We need to keep up your training, especially with Astor. It takes a great deal of inner strength to use magic, and your immortality gives you an edge she can't match. Her primary advantages are the power and favors she's gained as leader of the witches' council. Plus, she's been a witch for a long time with access to many grimoires and spells. That's where Astor can help. His knowledge of magic is ancient and deep," he comments. "I'm not sure I'd share your grimoire with her."

"She didn't really give me time to agree," I admit with a laugh. "She just assumed my answer was yes."

His lips lift in an incremental smirk. "Is that it?"

I wonder what it would take to get him to smile?

Not wanting to hide anything, I list the tasks. "Learn how to use all my powers. Find my witch heritage and the reason my mom hid me. Release the binding on my other powers, and hopefully, find my father. Track down the source of the assassinations and eliminate the threat. I think that's it."

His fingers grasp my chin, tilting my head back. "One more thing," he murmurs while staring down at me.

My heart skips a beat. Licking my lips, I rasp, "What?"

His eyes drop to my lips, hesitating, before continuing down to the base of my throat. "Tell me about the rune," he says huskily.

Blinking, I reply, "It was my prize for winning the Gathering of the Light." With a smug grin, I watch as shock steals over his face. I guess he's not the ice man he pretends to be.

"Rivan, the Rune Master, gave me a protection tattoo. It flares when I'm in danger, or if someone tries to use their powers on me. It's beautiful, isn't it?"

"You won the Gathering of the Light?" he challenges. "How? Very few outsiders have won it." The Fae pride themselves on the race they hold every hundred years. Winning is a testament to the winner's strength, courage, and intelligence.

Shrugging, I answer, "Solandis. She won it and helped me train for it. It was incredibly tough. I didn't think I'd make it, but somehow, I did. Didn't you win it, too? And Fallon?"

"Hmm...you're full of surprises," he comments, starting the car. He pauses for a second, his gaze intense, then continues, "Thank you for trusting me. I've already got Fallon and Daire checking into any contracts out on your life. Astor and Valerian will assist with your training. And I'm going to see if the supernatural archives mention your mother. Maybe we can trace her steps or find others who knew her."

"Thank you," I reply, reaching out to grasp his hand. "It means a lot to have friends looking out for me."

12

DAIRE

Solange rubs up against me like a cat in heat. Her skimpy silk and lace dress leaves little to the imagination, but then again, I've seen everything she has to offer. Beautiful from the tip of her dainty toes to the top of her glossy black hair, she's the epitome of vampire aristocracy. Besides her obvious physical traits, she's poised, graceful, and narcissistic, and of course, she holds an utter disregard for anyone who isn't a vampire.

She's been my girlfriend for the last two years. Her father, one of my father's closest friends, is constantly pushing me to offer her the Mate's Kiss, but I shudder every time I even think about it. I can't quite figure out why, either. If I wrote a list of the ideal traits I want in a partner, Solange checks every box.

Pouty lips caress mine. I glance down into her deep blue eyes. "Solange, who did you invite tonight?" The VIP area is packed with vampires. Friends and strangers fill the booths.

Her fingers walk up my tie, grab a hold of the knot, and she uses it to pull my head down for a deep kiss. Sighing, I give in, kissing her back with dedication and expertise. Kissing Solange is always pleasurable, but I'm restless tonight and not in the mood to play host to a bunch of sycophantic, overindulged, aristocratic vampires.

"Darling, why don't you go see if there's anything our guests need," I urge her.

With a pout, she reads the resistance in my eyes. "Fine, I'll go order some champagne for everyone. Your tab, okay?" She walks away without waiting for my reply.

As if she would ever think of paying for anything. Her family is wealthy, but she expects me to keep her in the manner she's become accustomed.

Blonde hair catches my eye below. It's Arden, laughing and joking while she serves her tables. She doesn't seem to have much in common with the witches I've met, but then again, she hasn't been indoctrinated into their warped view of the world yet, either.

Arden stirs my blood in ways I can't grasp. While certainly beautiful, it's not her beauty that attracts me, but her light. Her light shines like a beacon into the black hole of my heart. Shriveled long ago, I thought it to be dead and lifeless, along with Danica. Yet when I look at Arden, my heart opens an eye to stare at her, too, and gives a single solitary beat.

It's maddening, this new obsession. Solange would kill her. If Arden doesn't get herself killed by the witches first. Or her assassins.

Theron told us about their little meet and greet at Witchwood the other night and Arden's subsequent story-telling in the car later. She's playing a dangerous game with the witches right now by trying to uncover her past while hiding her power and making allies with witches behind Caro's back.

It takes every ounce of my will not to warn her away from them. The witches banished my mother when she became pregnant with me, as if the taint of a hybrid could be passed along like a disease. I snort and take a long sip of my old fashioned.

As I glance around downstairs, I notice several eyes following Arden. The light witches, dark witches, males of all races, and Merindah. Cocking my head to the side, I consider Merindah. Another enigma in the staff at The Abbey. She's watching Arden like a hunter staring at its prey, and I stiffen.

Watching Arden, Merindah quickly types a text to someone on her phone. The reply doesn't seem to make her happy, though, her face a thundercloud of emotions. She furiously types another message before dropping the phone in her pocket.

Theron needs to know there's something suspicious going on with Merindah. She's paying Arden way too much attention for a new colleague. I turn from the railing towards the elevators, but Solange stops me.

"My father is here. You need to come say hello," she drawls in that sensual voice of hers. Linking her fingers in mine, she pulls me over to where her father is standing with two young women, and distaste twists my mouth as I stare at him. Supposedly, he's happily committed to Solange's mother, but he plays hard when he's away from her. With a blank face, I wait for him to give me a nod of respect before I engage him in conversation. I make a mental note to mention Merindah to Theron later.

13

ASTOR

The incubus in me stirs as I watch Arden finish the latest bloodline test. Sometimes, I'm not sure if I'm the incubus or if it's a separate entity. I imagine it's similar to how a wolf shifter feels. The wolf is separate, and yet they are one and the same. My incubus is separate, always craving, and yet we're the same. It wants, and so do I.

Hunger and darkness swirl, desperate for a taste of her and her power. It sees only one and yet wants both. I shudder. She's everything we hate, I tell it and myself. She's light and balance, and her magic comes from the soul, not from sex and blood.

But every night, her power whispers to me, driving me to the edge while I mentally devour her from the VIP section. I don't know if I want to fuck or fight her.

Her long legs eat up the floor as she approaches, utterly gorgeous, and the incubus in me roars, panting for a sample. I ruthlessly hold myself in check.

"Hello, gorgeous. Ready to get your ass kicked?" I smirk.

"I just need a second, and I'll be ready," she replies offhand-edly, typing into her phone.

What the fuck? it roars.

Nobody dismisses me, man or woman. My incubus breaks the chains, filling the air with lust and desire. I watch, waiting for her response. Her nipples peak tightly under her shirt, and my cock hardens at this sign. Her hand moves down her body to her leg and...scratches? Then she shuffles, squeezing her legs together as if trying to soothe herself. Ah, that's more like it. My darkness reaches out to stroke her clit and hits a wall.

Seriously. What the hell is going on? it roars.

"Stop using your incubus powers," she commands. "They make me itch." She puts away her phone and crosses her arms. "I apologize. I needed to text Santiago to see if he would be willing to meet with me this week."

"Santiago? Why?" I demand, wondering why she has to meet the sneaky bastard.

"He's the head of bloodline six," she replies, as if that answers my question.

"And?" I prompt her.

"And he's the only one who can teach me how witches trans-figure," she states, narrowing her eyes at me. "Is that okay with you?"

"One of us should go with you," I grumble. "Don't go alone. And make sure you come back and tell me all about it. I've never transfigured nor seen a witch do it. I'd really like to learn more."

"I'll keep that in mind. Are we training today or what?" she reminds me.

Making a mental note to follow up with Theron about her planned visit to Santiago's, I jump into the training. "I need to figure out the best place to start. Do you have a grimoire or something you've been using to learn?"

She pulls a grimoire out of thin air and floats it over to me.

Holding my hand over the book, I quickly skim the spells, incantations, potion recipes, and other bits and pieces. The magic covers everything from the most basic of spells, like lighting fire, to more complex incantations, like power amplifiers. Okay, I think I know where to start, and she won't like it.

"You can do all of these spells? And well?" I demand.

"Yes, I've had plenty of time on my hands. Over three hundred years with nothing to do but train. Physically, mentally, with magic, without magic. Pick a spell," she challenges me.

"Share a power with me," I tell her.

"Done," she replies, lightning fast.

I frown, not feeling any changes. She walks over to stand directly in front of me and automatically, my mind strips the clothes from her body, my body and magic straining to be inside her. Her eyes narrow, and a wicked grin slides onto her face. She glances down at my body—my naked, rune-covered body. The one thing standing between her and I...is my hard cock, jutting out, saluting her.

Startled, I stumble back a step. Abruptly, the vision disappears. "What the hell?" I rasp, need making my voice tight.

"I thought an incubus like yourself would appreciate the spell," she drawls, a smirk lifting the corner of her mouth. "You can share anything, and it feels real. It's like an illusion or glamour created inside your mind, instead of perceiving it as an external vision. Did you like it?"

"I'd have liked it better if it had been real," I snarl, my cock aching to fuck her, and my grin broadens. She's not so innocent after all.

"How is a warlock different from a witch?" she asks, ignoring my statement.

"Witch magic comes from your soul, regardless of whether the witch is light or dark. I chose to shun my witch half and twisted my magic until it found another source. The source of warlock magic is primal," I cautiously explain. Witches loathe warlocks and the sources of their power. "Being part incubus, mine comes from sex and pain. Sometimes, I even use blood magic, although it's the most dangerous one."

"Can anyone use those sources?" she questions.

I hesitate, wondering why she would ask, before nodding. "Any person of power can use blood magic. But it changes them, introducing darkness and shadows into their magic where none existed. Blood is power. When you use blood magic, you sacrifice a bit of your power with the blood. Why are you asking?"

"I want you to teach me how to use blood magic," she drawls, as if she isn't asking me to introduce her to the shadows.

"Out of the question," a voice rings out behind me as Theron steps into the light. "Teach her everything else, but not blood magic."

"It's not your call, Theron," she furiously states.

Theron, hmm. Not Lord Theron? When did these two get so cozy? I sigh, telling my incubus to shut up.

"There's not much else I can teach her beyond her current knowledge," I counter. "She probably knows more witch magic than I ever learned. The only advantage I can give her is my knowledge of dark magic, which includes using blood. If you want her to outmatch the witches, she needs more than witch magic."

Frost lightly coats the walls while Theron paces.

He stops. "Fine, Fallon and I will watch. If she becomes consumed by the blood, Fallon will pull her out immediately and infuse her with light. You will not interfere. Do you understand me? I'm not joking, Astor," he demands, his face fierce.

"Yes, I won't interfere," I reply dryly, my heart pounding at the thought of sharing dark magic with someone of her power. My cock hardens further. Blood magic is intimate and dangerous. The more power you have, the greedier it becomes.

14

ARDEN

I glance at the frost climbing the walls and get a teensy bit worried. Theron is even calling in Fallon as...backup? I'm not exactly sure what he can do, because I haven't met him yet. In our investigation, the report stated Fallon's affinity for light is incredibly strong. Although he's a hybrid with an equal amount of light and dark in him, he shuns the dark.

Expecting a blond and ethereal elf, I'm astounded when a tall, dark-haired warrior strides confidently into the room, bright green eyes scanning his environment, before coming to rest on me. "Hello, I'm Prince Fallon. You must be Arden?" He holds out his hand in greeting.

"Hello," I reply, clasping his hand. Instantly, I gasp. It's as if I'm holding on to a live ley line. Magic and heat, snapping and crackling between us, flares wildly, then settles to a simmer. Warmth and light bathe my heart and soul, as if they've met their match. His eyes widen, and he eases his hand from mine.

I flush with embarrassment and take a deep breath. I'm not exactly sure what the hell just happened, but I'm going to ignore it for now. Taking a deep breath, I turn towards Astor, whose raised eyebrows tell me I didn't imagine my reaction to Fallon.

Shrugging, I square my shoulders. "Okay, my favorite dark warlock, teach me."

Astor glances at Theron and Fallon now whispering in the corner. "I've set up the tools on the table here." He motions to the black bowl, silver knife, quill, and paper waiting for me. "It's absolutely necessary you have a clear mind. If you're not focused, the source can take control and pull more power from you than you want to give. Take a seat. I want you to clear your mind and focus on what you want from the magic." Astor's chocolate brown eyes are fierce as he instructs me. "It's imperative your request is precise and not open to interpretation. The longer the source keeps you in the dark, the more power it drains from you. Okay?"

I murmur my agreement and close my eyes. After several deep breaths, I find my center and allow myself to drop into a relaxed, semi-aware state. Once I'm focused, I open my eyes and nod at Astor.

He picks up my hand, holds it over the bowl, and draws the knife across it. Blood wells up, and he tips my hand over to let it slide into the bowl. Picking up the quill, he hands it to me.

My blood stains the quill and paper as I tilt my hand to write. *Show me my assassins.*

Immense power invades my mind and blood. Images flash by too quickly to hold on to, and my head swirls. Nausea rises, but I grit my teeth and force it down. With a *whoosh*, I'm sucked backwards, falling into the dark, until suddenly, I'm standing in a massive cave.

Easily the size of The Abbey, the entire cave is lit up by sconces placed every few feet, fire burning in them. I turn in a circle, noting key details. I'm standing on a raised platform in a ceremonial chamber or something. A large tapestry hangs from floor to ceiling on the farthest cave wall, and I stop turning to study it.

The tapestry is adorned with a coat of arms depicting a black dragon holding a shield with four quadrants, each one displaying a picture. Fire, ice, shadow, and a crown. A motto arcs above the scene, *Courage Sans Peur.* Courage without fear. I don't recognize the coat of arms, but I'm guessing it's Valerian's. So this must mean I'm in the Kingdom of Dragons.

The air is cool, and I shiver.

Why would my assassins be dragons? My brow wrinkles when I think about what I wrote with the quill.

Yelling permeates my bubble, and I turn towards the noise. A crowd stands in the pit below, roaring, "Kill the witch! Kill the witch!" Several have slits in their eyes, telling me they're close to turning and confirming I'm in the presence of dragons. As if any doubt still existed. I snort.

Sensing movement to my right, I turn to see Theron, Valerian, Fallon, and Daire arguing with two gigantic men. I step closer to them.

Astor steps in front of me. He's trying to tell me something, but I can't hear his words, I can only see his mouth move. Worry pinches his features, and he holds a dagger tightly in his hand. Raising it above his head, I stare at him in disbelief. Is he going to stab me? The protection rune on my throat flares, warning of danger.

Something moves in my peripheral. My eyes cut to the right to find a huge male advancing towards me. Pain explodes in my chest, and I stagger. Looking down, I see the dagger in my chest, then my eyes find Astor's.

Why? I cry.

Relief and fear swirl in his eyes. My knees buckle as I slide to the ground. Grasping the handle, I try to pull the dagger out, but the blood is making it too slippery for me to grasp.

A roar fills the cavern, and the crowd quiets. Valerian drops to his knees beside me, the others standing behind him. Anguish fills his face as he cradles me in his arms, and I trace his features. The cold is seeping into me as fast as my blood is spilling out.

"My fierce dragon, it's okay," I assure him. The light fades from my eyes, and I'm left in darkness—pitch black, never-ending darkness. Confusion clouds my thoughts.

I call out, "Am I dead?" but nobody answers. I lie in the dark, unsettled.

Searing heat settles over me like a blanket, pushing out the cold. Light steals into the darkness like a thief, one step at a time, until arms reach down and pick me up, carrying me away from the dark.

I OPEN MY EYES, NOT TO THE DARK LIKE I FEAR, BUT TO SOFT light. I'm resting in a bed, covers pulled over me. Fallon sits in a chair beside the bed, a faint glow emanating from where our hands are joined, and warmth pulses inside me.

Astor sits behind him, his head in his hands. Fear and confusion war within me.

Did Astor really stab me? I think, questioning my vision.

Valerian slumps in a recliner in the corner, asleep, a frown marring his face.

Why were we in the Kingdom of the Dragons? I ponder all the possibilities for a couple of minutes.

Daire, leaning against the wall, flashes over, startling me, his ice-blue eyes bright with relief. "Thank fuck, you're awake. Why the hell would you do something so stupid?" His hands are clenched as he berates me.

Astor stands, shoving Daire to the side. "Arden, gorgeous. You gave me a hell of a scare," he rasps, his voice hoarse as if he's been yelling. "I couldn't reach you in the dark. We had to send in Fallon. What happened?" He reaches out to pick up my hand.

I pull it away quickly. "You stabbed me," I accuse. "Why the hell would you stab me?" Pulling my other hand from Fallon's, I use both hands to sit up. Pain lances through me, and I groan. My head pounds, and my body feels like I've been tackled by a dragon.

With a sigh, Fallon runs his hands over my temples and the pain in my head eases. "Nobody stabbed you," he reassures me. "Does this feel better?"

"Yes, thank you." I sigh softly.

Theron steps to my side, along with Valerian. "Why don't you tell us what happened?" he asks, cool and logical, as usual. "We saw what you wrote on the paper. Let's start from that point."

"I woke up in the Kingdom of Dragons, in a big ceremonial cave or chamber," I begin slowly, staring at Valerian to gauge his reaction, but he simply gives a fierce frown that doesn't tell me anything. I replay the scene, crystal clear images swirling in my brain, until I get to the end. "I don't understand what happened."

"Fuck! It's my fault. I should have been more specific. Blood magic is sentient. If the question is too broad, it will show you what you want, but not exactly what you were searching for, and it can result in a situation where you lose more blood. When someone stabbed you, it gained power from the blood you spilled. But it doesn't lie," Astor explains reluctantly. "If I was the one who stabbed you in the vision, it will happen. I'm not the source of your assassination attempts, though." His voice is dark, full of loathing. "I can swear a blood oath, if you want. I don't want you to fear me."

"No more blood magic," snaps Theron, his patience gone.

"I agree," Fallon says tiredly. "I don't have enough strength to save anyone else today."

Staring at him, I realize he saved me from the darkness. "Thank you," I murmur.

Fallon strokes his fingers over my face. "My pleasure."

Astor looks dejected. I lace my fingers with his. "We'll figure it out together, okay? On the bright side, I'm immortal. Stabbing me might hurt like hell, but it won't kill me."

He brightens. "You're right." Astor lifts my hand and places a kiss on it. "I'll work on trying to see your vision. We can figure this out before it happens."

I nod at Astor and then glance at Valerian. He's been quiet this entire time. "Are you okay? Can you guess why we would be in that particular chamber?" I inquire, asking a question I think only he can answer.

He stares at me, eyes roving over me intimately. "We'll talk later. Get some rest," he commands with a pat on my shoulder, then he strides out the door.

Theron's eyes follow him, before glancing at the others in silent communication. I don't know what they're saying, but I feel I've missed something big.

My eyes droop, and I slide back down into the bed.

I wonder whose bed I'm in? It feels incredible, I muse drowsily.

15

THERON

Relief pours through me as I stare down at Arden. When her body jerked violently and she fell to the floor, my heart stopped. I'd never seen blood magic react in that manner. When Astor uses it, it caresses him like a lover, making his body languid and sensual.

I rub my hand over my face in frustration. I'm responsible for protecting her, and yet I allowed this to happen. This should be the one place where she's safe. And instead of solving one of our problems, we've added another.

We have to figure out why Astor stabs her. Given it's in the future, our chances of solving this puzzle immediately are slim, but we also have the luxury of time to figure it out. And Valerian can help. Something in her story triggered him. He stiffened when she mentioned the chamber. I follow him out the door.

"What aren't you telling us?" I demand. "What's the significance of the chamber?"

Valerian ignores me, continuing to stomp down the hallway. Ice pours from me, sliding easily under his feet, causing him to slip. He crashes down to the floor, but it's as if his will drops with him. Valerian pulls himself to a sitting position against the wall and stares up at me, fear seeping from his very pores.

Alarmed, I slide down beside him. "The more we know, the better we can prepare," I remind him.

"We use the ceremonial chamber when the king is crowned, when he presents his mate to the clan, and when he dies. I've already got a crown, and I'm in the vision, so I'm not dead. It leaves one possibility," he replies hoarsely. "She's my mate." He pounds his head back against the wall. "A witch. My clan is going to go ballistic. Any other woman, and they would likely roar to the rafters with excitement, but a witch?" He shakes his head.

Arden is his mate? Startled, I whip my head around to stare at him. "Have you confirmed this?" I ask, waiting to hear if he's kissed her. While we often feel drawn to a mate, we can't confirm it until our souls reach out to entangle themselves with each other, which usually happens during a kiss or another physical act.

He shakes his head. "No, we haven't kissed," he admits. "But I'm drawn to her. More than Moira, in fact. I've been avoiding Arden since our last training session. I'm relieved she's immortal, but I can't fall for another witch. My clan will never accept her, not after the war I started when the dragons killed Moira and her entire family. Hell, her entire family line vanished overnight. All because I loved a witch."

I grasp his shoulders, forcing him to look at me. "I can't tell you what to do, but I'll remind you, a mate is more than love. Mate bonds are magic's way of influencing our destiny. To ignore it could be catastrophic." Patting him on the back, I rise and smooth down my suit. "Regardless, we're here to help her, and I expect you to do your part."

His mouth flattens into a scowl. "I remember. Now that there's a possibility she's my mate, my full power is at your disposal."

Satisfied, I walk away, my mind filled with the idea of Arden and Valerian as mates. Given how drawn to her I am myself, I'm surprised the idea doesn't upset me, but it doesn't. Instead, it feels like a piece of our giant puzzle is sliding into place.

ASTOR IS IN HIS LAB MUTTERING TO HIMSELF WHEN I FIND HIM. "What do you think happened?" I ask him curtly. "Why did it grab on to her so tightly?"

"I'm not sure. Blood magic is unpredictable. Although, I expected it to fight her a bit, I didn't expect it to throw her into a violent scene," he replies with a shiver. "I need to find out why it responded to her in that way, and I'm going to try to see her vision, get more clues."

"Keep me updated. Also, I spoke to Valerian," I say, sharing his insight. "If they're mates, it explains why we were in the ceremonial chamber, but not why you would want to stab her."

Astor winces. "I can't believe I would stab her. She's immortal. Stabbing her wouldn't kill her. So why? It's driving me crazy."

"Do you think it could be jealousy? If we're standing in the chamber, the likelihood they're mates is high," I comment.

"I couldn't hurt her. Fight with her, yep. Fuck her, definitely. Kill her...not a chance. She fascinates my incubus. It wouldn't let me. Hell, I'm fascinated by her, too," he admits. "But I hope she's Valerian's mate. He deserves someone like her—full of light, a warrior, a mate he'd be proud to have at his side."

My eyebrows raise at his declaration. Astor isn't known for his generosity to others, even to the cadre. We're close to him, but only to a certain point. Arden's influence on us is growing.

"Well, let me know what you discover. Try not to fall too deep into the dark," I implore him, knowing Astor's tendency to dance on the edge. "Keep Fallon close by."

He nods, turning back to the quill on the desk.

Watching him, I make a note to ask Fallon to stop by. Knowing Astor, he's already forgotten my request in his search for answers. At least this time, he's using his powers for something good.

16

ARDEN

Two days. Theron practically tied me to Valerian's bed for two entire days. I might have felt weak the first day, but by the second, I was fine. Convincing the stubborn Fae was another story. Fallon finally came to my rescue and told Theron I was completely healed. As soon as Theron agreed to let me out, I fled back to my hotel.

When I step off the elevator, I immediately hear my magical alarm blaring. It's an intruder alert, set to notify me of danger before I get close to my room. Slipping down the hall, I peek my head around the corner until I can see my hotel room. Light spills into the hallway. The intruder shattered my wards and left the door standing wide open. Pulling my phone from my back pocket, I shoot a quick text to Theron.

Arden: Someone broke into my hotel room. Can you send someone to back me up?

Theron: …

Theron: We're on our way. Do NOT go in there by yourself. Go to the roof. Valerian is flying to you and will be there in a minute.

Arden: I won't enter the room, but I'm not moving from this spot. If anyone steps out of that room, I want to see who it is.

Theron: Why can't you do as you're told?

Arden: Because I'm not a child. Stop distracting me. I'll see you soon.

I study the wards. They're shredded, as if the intruders weren't the least bit concerned with any alarms. I glance at the edges and notice they're still sparking magic, which means the intruders are still inside or we barely missed them. It also means they're powerful. Those wards were some of my strongest.

A soft click sounds behind me, and Valerian steps into the hallway. His black hair is windblown, and his amber eyes glow fiercely. He seems a little pissed—okay, a lot pissed—and I shiver. I haven't seen this side of him yet, but now I can see why grown demons shake in their shoes at the sight of him.

"Nobody's come out yet," I inform him. "I'm guessing they're not here anymore, but we didn't miss them by much." Pointing at the frayed edges of my wards, I show him the little magical sparks which indicate a recent disruption.

He pulls me back from the corner and steps in front of me. "Watch for Theron and the others. I'm going to see if anyone's in there."

I snort. "Not without me."

Valerian folds his arms and stares at me. He doesn't say a word, just gives me this fierce face. As if that's going to make me capitulate.

With a quiet chuckle, I cross my arms and match his stance. "You know I grew up with Vargas Karth as my guardian, right? Lucifer's executioner. The one that makes all the other demons wet their pants with one scowl. I became immune to hard stares and fierce frowns by the time I was six. Now, are we going in there together, or am I going in alone?"

Valerian sighs loudly in frustration. "Lass, try to stay behind me, okay? Dragons have much better armor than witches." He waits for my agreement, then motions for me to follow. Keeping the wall at our back, we slide around to the edge of the corner to my hotel room door. He stops and listens intently. Indicating he doesn't hear anyone, he peeks around the doorframe.

That's when I smell it—witch magic. There's a trap waiting for us. I quickly yank him back, pull up my shield and wrap it tightly around us. The spell releases, but it dissolves as soon as it hits my barrier, which tells me its intent to kill was weak. Confused, I pull the surrounding air into my lungs. It tastes of witch magic, but with a subtle hint of Fae. I know this person. Fury burns through me.

Once it's safe, I lower my shield, and we step into the room. It's completely trashed. They slashed the bed, ripped up the carpet, shattered the mirrors. Was the intruder searching for something? Too bad for them, I keep nothing but clothes in my hotel. I lock my important items in my vault, which is located in a pocket dimension and only accessible by Solandis and me.

Theron, Fallon, Astor, and Daire arrive a second later, their eyes assessing me from head to toe, relief and fury fighting for dominance in their expressions. Once they've reassured themselves, they spread out in the room.

"Upon entering, we triggered a spell, which my shield countered. But I was able to pick up the witch's signature. You and I met her at Witchwood, Theron. Amelie Von Dietrich." I stop and let Theron absorb this new information. "When we met her the other night, something kept teasing at my senses, but I couldn't quite grasp it. But her spell gave it away. She's part Fae, isn't she?"

Theron squats to pick up a bottle of my perfume from the floor and sets it on the dresser. "Yes, from an old family, based on what I could tell. Although, it's faint, maybe several genera-tions ago. Probably how they originally became masters of illu-sion and glamour. I don't understand why she would attack you."

"I don't know. She seemed unnerved at the meet and greet the other night. Probably because you were with me." I roll my shoulders, trying to ease the tension. "Another puzzle to solve. But I can trace this one to the source. I assume you'll want to be there?"

"Yes," Theron confirms. "And Astor, too. Like yourself, glamour is ineffective on him."

Shit. I'm still unnerved by the vision of him stabbing me and could use some distance. Which is precisely why Theron asked him to come along, as if I can't see through his little smoke screen. "Really?" I glance at Astor for confirmation.

With an absent nod, he explains, "The shadows permeate anything, real or not real. What do you want to take with you? I'll make sure they don't have any nasty surprises."

"Nothing, just burn it all. It'll be easier for me to get new clothes. I'll get more sent to my new place," I reply. No clothes and homeless. Great. My uneasiness with Astor takes a backseat to the rest of the crazy in my life. "Of course, now I need to find a new place."

Fallon interjects, "You'll stay with us. We can protect you better at The Abbey."

I glance at each one to see their reaction, but it's unanimous. Relief pours through me. Trying to work, protect myself from assassins, learn about my witch heritage, and keep up with my training is wearing me down. Moving into The Abbey would make life a lot easier.

A QUICK TEXT TO SANTIAGO PROVIDES US WITH AMELIE'S address. He demands an explanation, and an agreement he can join the discussion. He might be helpful, so I agree, although I keep the details minimal and don't mention Amelie's possible Fae heritage.

Instead of driving, Astor creates a portal to get us close to her house. When we step out a minute later, we're on a country road in front of a large estate. Behind the gates sits a house, its style reminiscent of the Fae, with delicate architecture and fanciful depictions of creatures and elements scattered throughout. Glamorous and beautiful, its picturesque setting is perfect as the ancestral home for witches of bloodline two.

The front door opens, and Santiago steps out. Of course he beat us here. In fact, I wouldn't be surprised if he'd come here immediately after our conversation. What I don't know is whether he's friend or foe right now. He strides towards us, his face solemn, and stops at the gate. I shift my stance in preparation, while Astor and Theron move in tight on each side of me.

Santiago's eyes narrow. "You didn't tell me to expect guests."

"Good thing we're not visiting you then, right? What's going on?" I ask, getting to the point. "We're not here to fight. If we were, we'd have brought the rest of the cadre. Amelie owes me an explanation, and I intend to get it from her. Tonight."

He tenses, then exhales. "She's in the drawing room, and I warn you, she's pissed you've come to her house, a councilmember's house, to question her."

"Well, if we're measuring pissed, I can assure you, I'll win that contest," I say coldly. "Please lead the way."

Santiago opens the gate and motions for us to follow him. When we get to the front door, he walks right in, but Theron and I pause. The door is carved with a montage of animals and scenes straight out of Fae fairy tales. I raise an eyebrow.

He cocks his head and studies the scene on the door. With a glance at me, he confirms the Fae origin behind the craftsmanship. He lightly brushes his fingertips across the door, probably trying to gain insight into the Fae who created them, then he frowns. Either he can't tell and he's irritated, or he can tell but the answer is unexpected.

When we enter the living room, Amelie is standing in front of the fire. She turns to face us. "Santiago said you're here to accuse me of a crime?"

I launch into my inquiry. "I don't like to play games. It pisses me off further. Tell me, why did you break into my hotel room?" I pause, but she says nothing. "Don't deny it. The trap reeked of your unique signature—a blend of witch and Fae, because of your mixed heritage."

"Don't be ridiculous, child. I didn't break into your hotel room," she drawls. "And I hate to inform you, but I'm not Fae. Only pure blood witches can serve on the council. I think they would have noticed if I wasn't pure."

"Lie," jeers Astor, the rune on his arm glowing.

Mmm…a truth rune. I want one.

I contemplate the rest of the runes on his arm and wonder what they do. I briefly recall his rune-covered body but remember little of the details. Of course, I couldn't stop staring at his cock, so that might be why I can't remember.

"Ahem." Theron glares at me while Astor laughs.

"How dare you use soulless magic in my house," Amelie shouts. "Get out."

Theron steps forward. "Fae always recognize other Fae, but given you're a few generations removed, you must take my word for it. A light summer Fae carved the scene on your door—my father's family. I recognized it immediately, just as I recognize you as a member of my family. Even diluted by a thousand years, blood can't be hidden. Now, tell us what's going on," he demands.

Amelie stumbles and moves to the couch. She glances at Santiago, who's standing there with a speculative gleam on his face. Her shoulders droop, and she reveals her secret. "We've been hiding our heritage for over a thousand years. If Caro or any of the other witches found out, they would banish us." She pauses and looks Santiago with pleading eyes. "I wouldn't have gone to Witchwood the other night to meet you if I'd known you were bringing Theron. I knew he would recognize another Fae, and I panicked. I thought if I scared you away, Theron wouldn't have any reason to come to witch ceremonies and our secret would be safe for another thousand years."

"Why would the witches banish you? I don't understand," I ask, frustration coloring my voice.

Santiago crosses over to the couch to sit with Amelie. "According to our archives, witches have banished hybrids for centuries. They're afraid mixing with other races will dilute our powers or eliminate them entirely," he explains.

I stare at him in disbelief. "Amelie is pretty powerful, I don't think your argument holds merit."

Amelie interjects, "According to the archives, we used to be significantly more powerful in the past. Each generation gets weaker and fewer are born. But if we mix with other species, witch power will cease to exist." She leans on Santiago. "I'm sorry. I'm sorry I attacked you. It's not you, I promise. I didn't want my secret getting out." Tears roll down her cheeks as she gazes steadily up at me. "What are you going to do?"

Uncomfortable, I glance at Theron. He gives me an impassive stare. I guess he's not going to give me advice. Astor, either, if I'm not mistaken, although, he at least looks pissed. It's a good thing I know Theron better now or my feelings would be hurt. I snort.

Squeezing the back of my neck to relieve tension, I stand there and think for a minute. "I'm not sure," I concede. "You attacked me and vandalized my hotel room. At a minimum, I expect you to pay for the damages." I pause for her agreement before continuing, "I'll keep your secret. For now. Not because I think you should hide your heritage, but because I need to figure a few things out first. Okay?"

Her mouth tightens in displeasure, but Santiago puts a hand on her shoulder and she relents. "Being a witch is all I know. It would kill me to be banished. If you decide to tell the council, especially Caro, please warn me so I can protect my family."

"Agreed. Here's my number. Send me a text when you've paid for the damages. We'll keep in touch. If you send anyone else after me or the cadre, I won't be held responsible for the wrath you'll incur, from me and from them," I warn.

Astor smiles darkly, and Amelie pales.

Theron turns to me. "Are you ready to go?"

I glance at Santiago, whose golden eyes are gleaming, and pause. Tingles run down my spine as an idea takes root. "I'll see you in a couple of days for our meeting," I remind him, eager to get out of here and do a little research.

He waves his hand in agreement, then turns back to Amelie. I guess we're showing ourselves out.

"Let's go home. It's been a hell of a long day, and I still need to order some clothes and stuff," I say tiredly.

Theron smiles, for like a microsecond. I think. Staring at him, I wait for him to do it again, but nothing. Ugh, I must be more tired than I thought.

17

ARDEN

I drag myself into the training room the next day, only to find Valerian and Astor waiting for me with devilish smiles on their faces. Hmm…it must be gang up on Arden day. Perfect. I crack my neck, feeling cranky.

My enemies are multiplying, and I'm not any closer to the answers I need. The witches have proven to be untrustworthy, exclusive, and intolerant. And I only have a few more days until the final two bloodline tests.

Annihilating Valerian and Astor would put me in a better mood, but I need to hit them dirty and quick or I can kiss my ass goodbye. These two are lethal on their weakest day. I return their smiles with my meanest, get fucked sneer, and Astor laughs.

Laugh while you can, warlock. We'll see who laughs last.

After cracking my knuckles, I pull two short swords out and get into a fighting stance. With my shield around me, I shout, "Bring it!"

A second later, a cyclone drops from the sky right on top of me as Valerian meets the thrusts of my swords with a claymore. Seriously, a claymore. Fucking Scot. Stepping out of reach, I change my strategy from attacking head on to a sneak attack. There's no way my two swords can compete with the power of a claymore, especially when it's wielded by a damn dragon. My only advantages are nimbleness and surprise, and I'll need to use tight, controlled movements against his powerful swings. Whirling around, we dance, the edges of our swords sharp, nicking each other here and there until blood coats the tips. I don't let my guard down for a second.

In the corner of my eye, I catch Astor, brow furrowed, as he tries spell after spell. Since he thinks I'm occupied, I use the same spell from the other day. Instead of naked bodies, he sees witches attacking me. His hatred of witches fueling his fury, he switches his focus from me to them, allowing me to redirect my attention back to the sword fight.

A thought pops into my head. Taking tiny steps back, I put more distance between us, waiting for the right moment. Valerian raises his sword, and I dive. Sliding neatly between his legs, I feel the air swoosh as his sword swings down, a centimeter from my head. Using a power spell, I punch him in the balls as I slide through and follow up with a power kick in the back of his kneecap. Goliath crashes to the floor, holding himself.

I don't have time to savor the moment. Jumping to my feet, I throw a sphere of light around Astor, scattering his shadows, leaving him open to my next attack. With a quick spell, I pull pheromones from my body, heighten them into a concentrated mist, and then douse him. The incubus responds, taking over from Astor, dropping and rolling, bathing in my scent.

Changing my angle, I rebalance in the center of the room, waiting for the intruder I sense. Looking around, my gaze locks on Fallon standing by the door. Shock blazes on his face for a brief second, before a full belly laugh escapes him. He salutes me, respect given from one warrior to another. A smile gracing his lips, he strolls over to check on Valerian, while I saunter out the door. No use sticking around for them to get up. I don't want them to ruin my good mood. Smiling, I head to my room to get ready for work.

THURSDAY NIGHTS ARE RAGING, AS USUAL, BUT I'M LOOKING forward to some space from my new friends. I've been living with them a couple of days, but I can already tell they're going to immerse themselves in my life. It's not a bad thing...yet.

Before I left to go downstairs for work, Theron stopped by to coordinate schedules. Not wanting to be rude, I told him, "Today, I kicked Valerian and Astor's asses, and now I'm going to work. Friday, I'm going to learn to transfigure. Saturday and Sunday are still up in the air. Next week, I'm going to learn how to heal. At the end of next week, I'll take the final two bloodline tests, maybe attend my placement ceremony. That's the plan for now. It's all I've got. If I add anything new, I'll get back to you." My lack of organization and planning appalled him.

I've got a plan, but it's not written on paper or anything. My plan is to keep following up on all the questions floating around in my head. Answers are surfacing, slowly.

Theron stalked off, muttering to himself, and I finished getting ready for work.

Here I am, an hour later, standing on the sidelines, waiting for my tables to be seated, when my shoulders start itching. I carefully scan my surroundings but notice nothing unusual until I look up. Theron, Astor, and Valerian stare down at me from the VIP section. Astor and Valerian smile broadly, while Theron is impassive, as usual.

With a scowl towards the protective bastards, I start thinking of new ways to bring them down. Unfortunately, I'm interrupted by a bunch of inhumanly beautiful men who are being seated at one of my tables. I smile up at the VIP section. This time, they're scowling.

I saunter over, barely refraining from licking my lips, to the table where the incubi wait for me to take their order. Clearing my throat, I ask them huskily, "Hello, I'm Arden. What can I get you?"

"Well, hello, baby girl. You can get me a shot of tequila and a lap dance. Preferably naked," a blond incubus calls out loudly, releasing a cloud of sex magic. They all laugh.

Damn. I hate being called "baby girl" almost as much as I hate dickheads. And forcing magic on a woman? Wrong witch, wrong move. "Gotcha, one shot of tequila for the blond bomber," I drawl, waving my hand in front of my face to disperse the cloud.

"Mmm...sassy. I like it, baby girl," he says sultrily. "Why don't you come over here and let Daddy take care of you?"

"I've already got a daddy, thanks," I reply before taking the orders for the rest of the table.

The asshole grabs my wrist.

Incensed, I pull my shield in tight until it's a second layer over my skin. "Let go of me." The control on my power loosens.

"I can make you feel so good," he rasps, stroking my wrist with his finger, subtly pulsing sex magic into the vein on my wrist. "I'm the son of the highest-ranking incubus, and I can make you come a hundred different ways. After you suck my cock and beg, of course."

I lean down to peer into his eyes, while I grab on to the finger at my wrist. Bending it completely backward, I hold it there. "And I'm the daughter of the executioner. I can kill you a hundred different ways. Want to play?"

His face pales, then he sneers, "You're not a demon, and definitely not Vargas Karth's daughter."

A hand cups my shoulder, and I look up. A blond giant stands behind me, shadows obscuring most of his face, except for his bright blue eyes. Smiling, I lean back. "I'll let you get acquainted with my brother while I go get your drinks."

Giving Callyx a kiss on the cheek, I leave him with the smarmy table of incubi. "Make them forget our conversation," I whisper.

Callyx narrows his eyes and nods. He takes a seat next to the dickhead while I go get their order.

I didn't realize incubi were such dicks. Astor pops into my mind. Well, except for him. He's an asshole, but not a dick.

Huh, I guess Astor is growing on me.

When I return, they all stand and bow to me. I motion for them to sit before I set down their drinks. "Will that be all, gentlemen?" I query, emphasizing the gentlemen part.

In unison, they nod their head yes. Callyx gets up and guides me over to his table as his friends wave from the dance floor. I've known them all since we were children, so I wave back.

"You should tell his father you saved his life. If he'd ruined my good mood, I'd have stabbed him and maybe cut one of his balls off," I jokingly tell him. "Enough. Tell me, how are they?" Homesickness wells up in me. I've never been away from Solandis and Vargas for this long, and I miss them terribly, and our home. I've called them a few times, but given we're all in hiding, we've limited our contact with each other.

Callyx pulls me into a bear hug. "That's from Dad." He gives me a kiss on my cheek. "That's from Mom." He punches me in the arm. "That's from me." He laughs. "They're good, still in hiding. Dad is pretty pissed he hasn't figured out who's trying to assassinate you. Mom is trying to reach the queen to ask for her help. They miss you."

I laugh and tap him on the chin with my fist. "I miss them." He looks wounded, and I shrug. "You're grown up, and you've been out of the house for a while. I'm used to seeing them every day."

"You worried us. I went by your hotel, and they said you'd checked out. Why? Did you find an apartment?" He folds his arms in front of him.

Let the interrogation begin. "Long story, but it was vandalized, and ultimately, too hard to defend. Too many people coming and going to put in a proper ward. Plus, I was going back and forth between here and there for training, then for work. It was crazy. It's easier now," I vaguely explain.

"Easier?" He reads between the lines, and anger crosses his face. "You're living here?"

"Shh, I don't want the entire world to know. Especially our friendly neighborhood assassins. I'm safer here than any other place. Do you disagree?" I challenge him.

Wiping his hand across his face in irritation, he scowls. "I don't like it, but I think you're right. Of course, you have to tell Dad." He smirks in anticipation.

Groaning, I agree. "I know. I will. Give me a day or three."

Seeing a silver ponytail flash by, I reach out and grab Meri's arm. Quick as lightning, she whips around and shifts her weight to the balls of her feet.

Interesting. Fight ready in less than a second.

"Whoa, tiger. I want to introduce you to my family. Callyx, this is my friend, Meri. Meri, meet Callyx, my adopted brother." I chuckle at the inside joke.

"Ha, I'm not adopted. You're adopted, remember?" Callyx interjects, turning his charm on Meri. "Hello, Meri. It's nice to know she's capable of making friends."

Meri seems frozen in place for a second, as if a movie is flashing in front of her eyes. She barely shakes his hand. "It's you—I mean, it's wonderful to meet you."

I blink at the expression on her face. She's mesmerized by

him. Turning to Callyx, I realize he's feeling the same. A voice calls out my name.

"Yep, okay. I've got to go take care of my tables. I'll leave you two to get acquainted...or reacquainted," I murmur, slipping away.

A few minutes later, I return as Callyx is getting ready to leave. "Are you leaving already?"

"I've got to check into something. Why?" he replies, his eyes following Meri.

I bite my lip, debating, but decide to ask him. "If you're around tomorrow, want to accompany me somewhere? I could use the backup."

"Sure, text me," he confirms. After giving me a hard hug, he walks out.

I glance over at Meri, who's watching him leave, then she pulls out her phone to text someone. Craning my neck, I try to see if it's Callyx, but he doesn't pull his phone out. I wonder what that's all about?

18

ARDEN

I'm watching Callyx leave, instead of where I'm going, when I bump into someone. "Oh, please excuse me." I glance up to find Daire's icy blue eyes staring down at me. "Daire. Are you okay?"

Straightening his cuffs, he slides an arm around the beautiful woman at his side. "Who was that demon?"

"Callyx Karth," I reply. "Why?"

The tension eases from his shoulders. "Karth, of course. The cadre wants to meet him. Maybe next time, you'll introduce us?"

I shrug. "Sure. I'm surprised you haven't met him, but then again, it's Callyx. Unlike Vargas, Callyx prefers to stay in the shadows, and Lucifer lets him." Turning to the woman, I introduce myself to her. "I'm Arden." I've seen them together a lot since I started working here, so I'm guessing she's his girlfriend.

She sneers down at my hand. "I'm Solange, Daire's girlfriend," she says curtly. "Daire, why are we talking to this witch? She isn't anyone important, is she?"

"This witch is under the cadre's protection, Solange. I'm checking to make sure she's okay. Put your claws away," he commands.

"What do you mean under the cadre's protection?" she screeches. "I've never heard of the cadre offering their protection to anyone. What does that even mean? Is she *living* here?" She puts her hands on her hips, her dark eyes flashing with fury, waiting for him to answer.

Daire's phone buzzes, and he looks up to see Valerian above him. "I've got to speak to Valerian for a minute. Why don't you go sit at our table," he suggests. With a flash, he's gone.

Exasperated, she gives a brief scream. "You. Answer my question," she demands. "Are you living here?"

"You should talk to Daire," I recommend, not wanting to get in the middle of these two. "I've got to cash out my customers." With a sidestep, I pick up the check from the table on my right and swipe their card on the tablet. After handing it back to them with a receipt and a pen, I'm walking to the next table when Solange grabs my arm.

I knock off her grip. "I told you, talk to Daire. I don't know you or trust you. Why would I tell you anything?"

She blurs in front of me, staring at me. "You'll tell me." The crowd falls silent, watching us. What she's doing is against the rules of sanctuary, but few will risk their neck for a witch. "But first, why don't you give me a little taste? You smell delicious." The rune at my throat flares in warning—she's trying to compel me.

A couple of guys in the crowd step forward, and she hisses at them. Nervously, they step back.

"Sorry, I'm not into girls, especially ugly ones. Meri, maybe. She's beautiful inside *and* out, but not you." I wrinkle my nose in disgust. "Go try your parlor tricks on someone else."

The crowd gasps, and the guys who stepped up to help chuckle.

"You bitch." She gives a deranged laugh. With a blur, she dives toward me, and I reach out and grab her by the throat in mid-air. Slamming her up against the wall, I hold her there. She's so tiny, she's like a gnat in my grasp. My temper frays.

"The first rule of attack is to know your opponent. You don't know me, and yet you assumed your vampire speed and strength would be to your advantage. Uh oh, it's not." I pull the sword hidden at my side. "The second rule is to prepare for surprises, which you clearly didn't do. Now you're in danger of having your head cut off." I take a deep breath, trying to get my anger under control. I can't kill Daire's girlfriend. It would piss him off. "I'm getting real fucking tired of people underestimating and attacking me. Now, what should I do with you?" I loosen my hand so she can speak.

"Daire!" she screams.

"I'm standing right here," he drawls. "What did you do to piss off Arden? Didn't I tell you I'd meet you at our table?"

"Are you going to stand there and let her treat me this way?" She cries, fake crocodile tears rolling down her cheeks. "Obviously, she's using magic to enhance herself. Who knows what spells she's planning to use on me."

"A spell? I'm more likely to use my sword to cut off your head so I don't have to hear you screech anymore," I snap. The crowd whispers. Remembering where we are, I drop her to her feet. I hold the tip of the sword at her throat. "You're lucky we're in a sanctuary. The next time you attack me, I won't be so lenient."

Valerian stalks over and grabs the hand holding the sword. "Lass, I think your shift is over. Let me get you a drink."

"I deserve one after Daire made me clean up his mess," I snarl. "How he can date someone so stupid is beyond me."

A shriek sounds behind me, and I watch while Daire reaches

out to wrap his arm around Solange's waist. He peers down at her, tucks a piece of hair around her ear, then leans down to whisper to her. With a roll of my eyes, I turn and motion to Valerian.

"Lots of alcohol. Something strong," I tell him.

19

ARDEN

Pixies hammer loudly in my brain, and I grasp my head with both hands to hold it together. What the hell did I drink? I groan. It's been a long time since I've been this hungover. Potion. I need a potion for the pain, but I can't open my eyes. I try to pull the pillow over my head, except I'm not lying on a pillow. I'm lying on something warm and hard and big.

The smell of a bonfire on a crisp night has me opening one blurry eye. Smooth brown skin comes into focus. Skin means a body, and not my pale body, either. Dread rolls through me. Forcing the other eye open, I see a familiar headboard. What am I doing back in Valerian's bed? And with Valerian?

The bed shifts, and a hand drops on my waist, pulling me tighter to the warm body beneath me, skin meeting skin. What the hell happened to my clothes? Panic rises.

"How are you feeling this morning, lass?" Valerian asks gruffly. "You drank a hell of a lot of whiskey last night. I think between us, we finished the bottle. I'm getting up to get a glass of water and a potion, do you want one?"

"Yes," I croak, parched.

Valerian shifts me to the side and stands. The sheet slips down, and I gather my courage and peek. Boxer briefs. Black, tight-fitting boxer briefs and a rock-hard ass. Any other time, and I'd stop and admire the sight before me, but I'm so relieved to see clothes, I can't even think about what's under them. It doesn't mean something didn't happen, but it's a start.

Shifting in the bed, I wait until he's in the bathroom, then lift the sheet. My black lace bra and panties are...on. My heart thuds in my chest. Nothing big happened. I sigh with relief...I think. I drop the sheet when I hear the door open. Scooting up in the bed, I tuck the sheet around me.

He places a glass of water and a vial of potion in my hand. "You're a lifesaver," I whisper, not wanting the pixies to start jackhammering in my skull again. My fingernail pops the cork off the potion, and I pour it down my throat, then drink the entire glass of water.

He takes the empty glass and sets it down on the nightstand, while I lean back and close my eyes. It usually takes about fifteen minutes for the potion to remove all traces of a hangover. Fingers slide into my hair, massaging my scalp.

Mmm...that feels good. I drift peacefully.

He stops massaging. "It's been ten minutes, lass. Better?"

"Yes, thank you," I reply, opening my eyes. "What happened last night?"

"Well," he says with a grin, "I opened my best bottle of whiskey, and you almost drank me under the table. Only Fallon or Astor comes close to drinking as much as me, but you quickly passed their limits."

"I'm used to this homemade demon whiskey Vargas brews. It's like fire going down and carries a hell of a punch. Your whiskey felt smooth as glass, in comparison," I explain. "Why are we in your bed, half-naked?"

"You tried to take advantage of me. After you took off your clothes, you climbed in my bed and insisted I take off mine," he says fondly, scratching his chin as he thinks about last night. "Then when I caved, you promptly passed out. I joined you, covered us up, and fell asleep."

Heat covers me from my face to my chest as embarrassment crawls over my body. Clearing my throat, I confirm, "So, nothing happened between us. We drank, I stripped, then passed out?"

"Aye, lass. I wouldn't take advantage of you in that state. In fact, we sort of need to have a conversation before anything happens between us," he says reluctantly. "First, I need to tell you a story."

Scooting up, I cross my arms over my knees and wait.

Valerian reaches into the nightstand beside the bed, pulls out a small painted picture of a beautiful woman, and hands it to me. The painter easily captured her sparkling blue eyes and auburn hair, along with a quirk in the corner of her mouth, which seems to suggest she was amused when sitting for the painting.

I scrutinize Valerian. A nightstand picture is serious. It's within reach for a reason.

Pacing the room, his hands behind his back, he starts his story. "Her name was Moira MacAllister. She was a witch and I loved her, very much. We grew up in the same small town. Her family had lived in the village for as long as I can remember. I paid little attention, until one day, I saw her playing in the field with other children. Her laughter filled the air, and all I wanted from that day forward was to be near her. Whenever I could get away from my duties, I went to her. First, we were friends, sharing secrets and adventures." He pauses, eyes cloudy with memories. "Until one day, I looked up and saw a grown woman, and my feelings changed from sweet friendship to desire and love. Nervous I'd ruin our friendship, I waited weeks to tell her. When I finally told her, she laughed and told me she'd almost given up on such a dunce." He laughs in remembrance.

"For the next year, we would sneak away, spend hours loving each other, then sneak back to our homes. We knew we needed to tell our families, but it was as if we could sense the timing was wrong. So we held on to our secret." Valerian sits down on the bed and glances at the painting before continuing, "She gave me this picture for our one-year anniversary. It meant the world to me."

Love shines in his eyes, and it's breathtaking. A thousand years later, and he still feels love for this woman. Envy pinches my heart.

"I left the painting on my nightstand. That night, my father, who never visited my room, decided he had to speak to me. When he saw the painting, he knew. He asked me if she was my mate. I told him I loved her and intended to marry her, but she was not my mate. He demanded I stop seeing her, and I refused. Incensed, he left, locking me in my room with guards posted." His voice tightens with anger. "It took me an hour to get past them, but by then, it was too late. My father had already killed Moira."

Valerian drops his head into his hands. "Blind rage filled me. This man, my father, killed the brightest light in my world. Why? Because he was the King of Dragons, and he refused to allow me, his son and the future king, to marry a witch. And to be sure her family wouldn't retaliate, he ordered his guards to kill her family, which they did. Not because it was right, but because he commanded it." He glances at me nervously. "So I took his kingship away. I murdered him and all those who helped him, dragged my father's lifeless dragon into the chamber, took the crown, and placed it on my head. From that point on, I was King of Dragons." His eyes, full of anguish, stare at me, trying to gauge my reaction.

Tears sting my eyes, for him, her, their families, and even his father. Sitting up on my knees, I pull him into my arms and squeeze tightly. He gives a large exhale, yanks me into his lap, wraps his big arms around me, and holds me tightly. Finally, I lean back and look at him. "I'm so sorry."

Tears fill his eyes at my response. "Thank you, lass," he says gruffly. "Besides the cadre, the entire world thinks my ambition drove me to murder my father, to become King of Dragons. My clan hates me. If they could get rid of me, they would. For a long time, I believed I deserved it, until I met the cadre. They saved me, convinced me that neither Moira nor I deserved it."

"I could go punch a few of them in the balls for you," I offer.

He gives me a mock scowl. "That's not even remotely fucking funny. It hurt!"

"Of course it did, big baby. I needed to put you down hard and fast. I wasn't going to last long against a fucking claymore," I snarl, teasing him to help lighten the mood.

A sheepish grin covers his face. "I can't help if my sword is big and long and needs two hands to hold it."

Pushing back, I fall on the bed, groaning. "Stop. You're terrible." His eyes travel down my body, desire flaring in his eyes. I pull the sheet up around me, and he smiles. I grasp his hand. "Thank you for telling me about Moira. It means a lot to me that you would share this part of your history." Startled, a thought occurs to me. "Did you say MacAllister?"

"Yes, Moira MacAllister. Why?" he questions.

"I'm not sure yet. I've got a hunch, but I need to do a little research," I tell him, my mind racing to integrate this latest information with my witch knowledge. "Do you know if there were any other MacAllister witches, besides her immediate family?"

"I believe so, but it was a long time ago. And I've never met another since," he replies. "Thank you for listening, lass. You're welcome to stay, but I think you mentioned last night you had a meeting today?"

"Shit, what time is it?" I glance at the clock and notice it's about noon. "Yep, got to go. We'll talk later." I slide out of bed, wrap the sheet around me, and grab my clothes from the floor. I bend down and give him a kiss on the cheek. With a wink, I open the door. "Thanks for last night."

I close the door, turn around, and bump into Theron. His eyes take in my rumpled hair and my lack of clothes, and I'm sure he heard my comment to Valerian. I want to slide to the floor in embarrassment. I've only been living here a few days, and I've already spent the night with one of them. I open my mouth to explain, but without a twitch of an eyebrow, he walks past me. Probably for the best. I'm late anyway.

20

ARDEN

Callyx is standing outside of The Abbey texting when I walk up. I give him a quick hug and open a portal to Santiago's. We step through, and within seconds, we're in front of a sprawling Spanish-style villa, the white adobe walls and terracotta roof a nod to their heritage in a sleek, luxurious package. Santiago is waiting at the gate.

"Arden, welcome. While I didn't expect you to come alone, I also didn't expect you to bring a demon. Unfortunately, I can't allow your companion into my house," he states firmly.

Exasperated, I sigh. "Hello, Santiago. I'm not here to wage war. Callyx is here for my protection. It was him or Astor, and I thought you might feel Callyx was the better choice. Or was I wrong? I can go back and get Astor?"

Santiago relents. "Fine, but we'll stay outside. I'm not having him in my house."

I nod in agreement. "Works for me. Thank you."

Once inside the gate, Santiago leads us to an area in the grass beside the pool. "Before we start, I'd like to know why you think you have an affinity for my bloodline?"

"I've never transfigured, if that's what you're asking. Nor healed someone. But if my test is negative for both those bloodlines, I want to be sure it's because I don't have an affinity, not because I don't understand how to use the powers," I explain.

"It's unlikely you have an affinity with my bloodline, unless you know something I don't?" Santiago raises an eyebrow in question.

"Why?" I ask, evasive in my reply.

"My family purposely limited our integration with the rest of the families. In the beginning, it was because the power was too volatile. The slightest emotion could trigger a transformation. Imagine having an argument with a friend and accidentally turning into a wolf." He pauses before continuing, "As time went on, though, we realized the light was angling to take over the entire coven. We made a family pact to avoid any relations with the other bloodlines. And there have been many, many requests. Even now, Caro would like nothing more than for her daughter to marry me and bear a child with all six bloodlines."

I should be shocked, but I'm not. Caro wears her ambitions like diamonds, proudly around her neck. "Well, this might be a waste of time, but if you don't mind, I'd like to try it anyway," I respond.

With a decisive nod, he begins his explanation. "Unlike most witch powers, the ability to transform comes first from the head. You must carefully imagine, in the most minute detail, the creature you want to become. If you accidentally forget to add a body part, it will be missing when you transform. Take your time and build a picture. Once you identify all the details, we'll continue."

Tilting my head to the side, I consider all my options. Probably best to choose something less predatory and potentially easier to control. When a unicorn pops into my mind, I realize it's perfect. When I have all the details in my mind, I give him a nod.

"Now, this is the hard part. To transform, you must infuse the image with spirit, not power. Spirit gives the animal life, making it more than an illusion or a glamour. It shares a piece of your soul." Santiago lets out a long exhale. "Reach into your soul and pull a small thread from it. Wrap the thread around the image in your head, then will the animal to accept your spirit and merge with you."

Closing my eyes, so I don't see Callyx's worried face, I envision my soul, the place where my power and spirit reside. With a tug, a piece of thread comes loose. Taking it in my hand, I picture it wrapping around the unicorn, but nothing happens. Changing tactics, I stroke the unicorn's neck and mane with the thread and push my desire to become one with every pass of my hand. Light bursts from the unicorn in a wave, swallowing me whole. The light, filled with intense heat, transforms me into the unicorn, one molecule at a time, until I stand there in front of them.

Shock and fear wage war on Santiago's face, while Callyx is smug. Of course, he's been around me all my life and knows I see limits as flimsy barriers.

I neigh, stomp with excitement, then nudge Callyx. With a laugh, he snaps a picture on his phone.

Santiago recovers quickly. "To transform back, think about the process in reverse. See yourself, using the same extreme attention to detail. Spool the thread back into your soul."

Picturing myself with precise detail is more difficult than I expect. I can barely remember my clothes or how I fixed my hair today.

"Don't worry about unnecessary details like clothes or makeup. Any clothes will work. I typically use the same image of myself each time to make it easier. For now, concentrate on the details of your body, the most important parts," Santiago suggests.

With a deep breath, I complete the picture of myself and throw on my favorite jeans and long-sleeve T-shirt for simplicity. Intense heat encompasses me, and I'm suddenly me again. My hands run over my body, needing reassurance I didn't forget something, like a nose. Finding everything where it should be, I exhale.

"That was…intense," I confess, rolling my shoulders to ease my tension. "I'm not sure I'll be comfortable using transfiguration unless I have a lot of practice." Exhaustion rolls over me, and I stagger. Callyx steps close and holds me up for a second.

"It's remarkable you have the power at all," Santiago says with a frown. "I can only think of one possibility. My great-great-great-grandfather loved the ladies, and he was the black sheep of our family. He's the only one I can think of who might have flouted our rules. His journals are in the attic, but it will take time to dig through them."

If that's the case, he must have had an affair with my mother's mother. With a shrug, I figure it's best to let him figure it out.

"Promise me you'll keep this from Caro," he demands. "She's already looking for ways to control all the bloodlines. The light needs the dark for balance, but she doesn't understand the concept. To her, the greater good of the coven relies on its alliance to the light. Dark isn't evil, it's the concept of free will. But to Caro, free will must be squashed in order to find the best way forward for the coven. If she aligned the entire coven, we would be more powerful, but she manipulates everything to the light's advantage. She even installed her husband as leader of bloodline four."

"What do you mean? Who's supposed to be the leader of bloodline four?" I ask.

"His name is An Lee. You might have noticed him hanging

out with my daughter. The Lee family has a handful of members left. Caro's husband, Adam, is a Lee, but she made him take her last name. Technically, a Lee is head of bloodline four, but Adam is not the most powerful. His sole claim is a powerful wife. I don't know what she did to make the Lee family concede the leadership to him, but she'll never let them take over again." Santiago's anger fills the air.

"To be clear, the six founding families are Pennington, Martinez, Lee, Perrone, Dietrich, and Ivanov?" I query.

"Correct," he answers.

Interesting. Then who were the MacAllisters? Another unanswered question, but I might have a source to find the answer. With a smile towards Santiago, I answer his previous question. "Thank you, Santiago, for teaching me to transform and for the information. I wish I could promise not to tell Caro, but I've got two more bloodline tests coming up, so she'll find out then. Maybe you could suggest that she hold the last two tests and the placement ceremony at the same time? Then you can be there, and Caro won't be able to suppress the knowledge from the coven." It might be the best way to control the situation.

His shoulders droop, but he agrees. "I'll see what I can do."

CALLYX STOPS ME ON THE WAY OUT. "ARE YOU OKAY? YOU'RE pale."

"Transforming is draining. It uses a lot of power," I explain. "But this afternoon was enlightening. I'm ready to get back and do some research."

A roar comes from behind, and I turn to see a panther sprinting towards us. My hands prepare to fight, but I notice the golden eyes and hold back. It's Santiago, but why is he charging us?

Callyx's battle cry rings out. I turn and quickly bring up my shield against an attack. There must be over twenty assassins this time. I see a couple of shifters, a warlock, a troll, a vampire, but I can't make out the others as they attack. My mind shifts into battle mode, and I pull my twin swords.

Callyx's shadows roll off him in waves, and it helps even the fight as several assassins fight illusions only they can see.

There's a blur to my right, and I strike out. The vampire's head falls to the ground, but savoring the win has to wait, because the troll is locked onto me. I've never fought a troll, and I can't recall their weaknesses, but their strengths are easy to find. They're big, bigger than Valerian, and quicker than I'd expect. His fist catches the edge of my jaw, and I fly into the fence.

With a quick shake, I jump up and charge him. Bringing one sword up above my head, I keep his eyes distracted and pull the same move on him that I did on Valerian yesterday. A quick slide between his legs and a power punch to his balls brings him to his knees. He's now at my level. One quick stroke with my sword, and his head rolls off his body.

A searing pain in my leg has me turning to face a new threat. A wolf, claws extended and dripping with blood, my blood, stands behind me. I don't look down to see the shredded muscles of my calf. My feet find their battle stance automatically, and I wait. We circle each other, the wolf looking for a way past my defenses, while I do the same.

Callyx shouts, and I tense, just as a huge weight hits me from behind. I slam to the ground, pinned beneath a couple hundred pounds of wolf.

Shit! A diversion.

A piercing scream fills the air, and I'm suddenly free from the weight on my back. I glance to the side as I jump up, finding a black panther with the wolf's neck between its jaws.

A howl brings me back to the one remaining wolf in front of me. I strike out with my sword, catching it in the side, and it launches toward me. I drop one sword in order to infuse my hand with magic, but it lands on top of me. I reach out and grab its throat, using power to keep it off me. Jaws snapping, it strains to reach my throat. Claws dig into my side, and furious, I scream, "Motherfucker!"

With magic, I swap the sword in my other hand for a dagger. I look to my right, as if I see something, waiting until the wolf turns its head, then I bring my left hand up, and stab it in the throat. It rolls off me, swiping with its paw to get the dagger out. I leap up, grab the sword I dropped, and swing. Another head rolls to the ground.

Shaky, I scan the bodies. The rest of the assassins lie scattered around us. Callyx, Santiago, and I assess each other, blood dripping from our wounds. I sway, and Callyx puts his arm around me and picks me up.

"Thank you," he says firmly to Santiago. "I'll take Arden to The Abbey. Will your men be able to take care of the bodies and help you inside?"

Men? A couple men, holding bloody swords, come up to Santiago. They must have joined the fight, but I didn't notice.

"Yes, we'll be fine," he tells Callyx. "Go, take care of her. I don't want her to die. My gut says we need her more than ever." He nods at me before turning to his men to issue orders.

Callyx opens his mouth, but I slam my elbow into his side. Angry, he glares down at me, and I give him a slight shake of my head. Rolling his eyes, he opens a portal and takes us back to The Abbey.

21

DAIRE

I'm arguing with Solange on the phone when Callyx stumbles into The Abbey with Arden in his arms, blood pouring from both of them. Fuck. I shout for Theron as I end the call, then take Arden from Callyx. He slides to the floor when Theron appears.

"What happened?" Theron strides over to check on Arden.

Callyx wearily answers, "Assassins."

Theron checks Arden's wounds. "She's unconscious, and probably entering a healing stasis. The wounds are pretty bad, but let's see if she can heal herself first."

I pull her closer to me. "I'm going to take her upstairs. Can you grab him?" I sneer at Callyx, pissed he didn't protect her. He's one of Lucifer's best? I may need to check and make sure dear old Dad hasn't gone senile.

Theron easily picks up Callyx and throws him over his shoulder. Callyx grunts, and Theron smirks. Humph, guess he feels the same way I do.

Cradling Arden, I summon the elevator and wait for them to join us. The elevator closes and, with my command, takes us to Arden's room. I lay her gently on the bed. My incisors lengthen as they take in the amount of blood seeping from her wounds, and I breathe deeply. "Theron."

He sets Callyx down on the couch and walks over to the bed, where he waves his hand to clean the blood from Arden, but it keeps flowing. Cloths appear over her wounds, then he takes my hands and places them on top of the cloths. "Until her wounds heal, hold these cloths over them."

Not wanting to give in to temptation, I jerk my hands away and step back. "I can't."

"You can and you will," he demands. "She needs you. I need to find Astor so he can check them for any spells."

Swallowing, I exhale and step forward. Placing my hands on her sides, I put pressure on the cloths to stop the bleeding, then I tell him, "Be quick."

Theron doesn't reply as he walks out the door.

Avoiding her wounds, I stare down at her face. A bruise is darkening on her cheek, and rage fills me. Why is someone sending assassins after her? When we find out, they better hope heaven helps them, because the Underworld is my domain, my playground, and it's a brutal, unforgiving place.

It looks like one of her side wounds has stopped bleeding. I lift the cloth to check, but a whiff of her blood has me putting it back. A slight tremor makes my hand shake, and I lift it in wonder. It's been a long time since I strained my control this much.

Arden shifts, and I reach up to push her shoulders back down on the bed. My hand strays to her cheek, softly skimming the bruise. She moans, and I freeze. It must hurt her. With a featherlight touch, I trace her cheek. She's so beautiful, but more than that, she's a warrior. Admiration for her courage spills out of me.

My hand, hovering over her cheek, begins to glow. Startled, I hold it there, watching as the bruise slowly recedes, then disappears. Tears fill my eyes. I'm healing her. I haven't healed anyone in over a thousand years. When the darkness took over, I thought the power had fled permanently.

Arden moans and opens her eyes. Her hazel eyes stare up at me with gratitude. "Thank you. Never step in front of a troll's fist," she advises and laughs.

Anger surfaces, but I push it down. "He better be dead," I tell her.

"Missing his head, in fact," she replies. Shifting in the bed, she groans. "I don't suppose you could help my wounds heal faster?"

"I can try." With both hands, I hover them above the wounds on her sides. Glowing, they knit the punctured skin closed. "What happened here?"

"Shifter. Wolf. He got the back of my calf, too. Although, I think it's healed," she says, flexing her leg.

With a glance, I see smooth skin on the back of her leg. "It's healed," I confirm.

Arden stares at me speculatively. "I didn't know you could heal. Your dad never told me. I assume the power comes from your mother? She was a witch and a healer, right?"

"Yes. I could heal small animals as a child, but the power left me right before Danica…died." My voice is tight as I finish that statement. I never speak about my sister. Although I saved her, she was never the same afterwards. "Being unable to heal seemed a fitting punishment for not saving her."

"Your father told me you saved her from the demon gang who kidnapped her," she replies with a frown. "Is that not correct?"

"I killed them all and brought her home. But she was never the same. For a year, she wouldn't leave her room. She alternated between terror and rage, unable to cope with the things they did to her. Her body was whole, but her mind was broken.

She would scream for me to heal her. Even if she weren't already healed, I couldn't have done anything more. The power deserted me after I killed her kidnappers. She didn't believe me, thought I was punishing her for flirting with a demon." I remember every day as if it was yesterday. Anguish fills me, and I feel as helpless now as I did back then. "She was afraid they would come back for her. Afraid I was lying about their deaths. She would rage at me for hours. After all, I was part demon. I probably covered it up to appease my father. I assured her over and over they were dead, but she didn't believe me. Nothing I did or said worked. I visited her regularly, trying to get her to forgive me. The day before my last visit, she walked out of her room and into the lake. Her body floated up the day I arrived." I stare down at my glowing hands, then snuff out the power. I can't bear to think about Danica or that period in my life.

Arden reaches out and grabs both of my hands in a tight grip. Her voice is fierce as she tells me, "Your sister wasn't herself, you must know that. Lucifer says she worshipped you. Do you think she would want you to remember her ending or her beginning? Lucifer spoke about her often. He said she was filled with light and love. Is that true?"

I smile in remembrance. "She giggled all the time. And she was so good, so pure. All light and love, like my mother. Her joy was infectious, making me laugh all the time."

"Then hold tight to that vision of her. I'm glad you killed them, but don't punish yourself for what happened. Do something about it. You're Lucifer's heir. With your power, you can make sure it doesn't happen again." She squeezes my hands. "Your sister should be your inspiration. Other families don't have the resources you do to find their loved ones in the Underworld."

I stare intensely at her hand on my arm, before covering it with mine. "You're right. I can help others by putting in place better laws and protection and punishments. I'll speak to my father. Thank you."

"I'd like to ask you for a favor, for your help. Only if you want to help. If not, I've got other resources," she babbles, and I want to laugh. "My last two bloodline tests are coming up, and one of them is healing. I need to know if I can heal someone. Will you teach me? If you don't want to, I can ask An Lee. Actually, that's what I'll do. Forget I said anything." She bites her lip and looks away.

"Yes, I'll teach you," I reply solemnly. "Healing is important to your health and to others. You never know, one day, you might have to save one of the cadre."

Callyx groans from the corner and stands. His eyes glance from our clasped hands to my face. Raising an eyebrow, he silently asks me what the hell I'm doing holding her hand. He forgets I'm a Prince of the Underworld. I don't have to explain myself to him.

"I've got to go. Lucifer is requesting my presence. I'll pass along the assassin information to Vargas and see if he can pick up any leads," he states. Striding over, he kisses her forehead and uses his hand to knock mine away from her.

I stand. "How dare you touch me?"

"Don't you have a girlfriend?" Callyx reminds me. "Don't mess with my sister."

"Your sister can take care of herself," I tell him.

Angry, he huffs, but Arden sharply calls his name and he deflates. With a growl, he stalks towards the door.

Theron walks in with Astor, who insists on checking Callyx before he leaves. Thankfully, no spells cling to him or Arden.

After Callyx leaves, I pick up her hand again, needing the light to stave off the darkness. She gives my hand a squeeze and smiles up at me, and my heart gives that one unsolicited beat.

22

FALLON

I head to Arden's room when I get Theron's text. Apparently, there's been another assassination attempt. Fuck! I sweep my hand down my face in frustration. I haven't been able to find one lead to follow. No matter where I send inquiries, nobody has information.

Which reminds me...Cormal has been extremely quiet these days. For the criminal king of the supernatural, this is uncharacteristic, since Cormal is usually the first one to bargain with me. He always has some tidbit of information to share or to use as leverage. I shoot him a text.

FALLON: ARE YOU LOSING YOUR TOUCH?

Cormal: Prince Fuck You, nice to hear from you. I've lost a dozen men trying to get this information.

Fallon: So that's a yes?

Cormal: I've got nothing. Every time I think we're getting close, I find one of my men, dead. Whoever is behind this is powerful. There are only a handful of supernaturals with this kind of power, and they've all got royal blood.

Fallon: I see. Keep your ears open but send no more men.

Cormal: This is personal now. I don't give a fuck if they're royalty. I'm going to hunt this bastard down.

Fallon: Let me know what you find.

DREAD TIGHTENS MY GUT. WHOEVER'S BEHIND ARDEN'S assassination attempts, they've got an endless supply of power, wealth, and resources at their disposal. The good news is we can rule the witches out. While they have power and wealth, they don't have the endless supply of resources it requires to repeatedly send out teams of assassins. That leaves her father's side.

Entering Arden's room, I notice Daire is sitting close to Arden on the bed, her hand clasped in his. Callyx is on his way out, so I step aside to let him leave. One of his shadows slithers out to probe me, but recoils when it reaches my aura. Like Astor's, they abhor me.

A step to the side of the bed brings me closer to Arden and the potent smell of blood. I'm surprised Daire is able to sit this close to her. Without thinking, I lean down and kiss her forehead. She glances up and smiles at me.

Theron and Daire are fussing, trying to get her to stay in bed, but she's insisting she's healed.

"You're a fast healer, Arden, even for an immortal," I say, puzzled. "Were you not as injured as Theron thought?"

"Daire healed me," she explains, squeezing his hand. "Now can I please get up? I need to think, which means I need to pace."

Theron motions for Daire to move. "Stubborn witch," he mutters.

"I heard that," she spits out. "I'm three hundred and twenty-eight years old, not twenty-eight, and quite capable of assessing my own health."

Theron snarls, then crosses his arms. "Well, I'm one thousand eight hundred and thirty-three years old. At my age, I certainly know more than you do."

"Damn, you're old. Are you all that old? The air is stale around here, like moldy bread. It could explain the crankiness factor," Arden teases. "Well?"

"I'm two thousand and six. Second oldest here. But I'm not cranky," I protest.

"Hmm...time will tell, Fallon. Who's the oldest?" she asks.

"Valerian," we all state in chorus.

"I'm two thousand seven hundred and seventy-eight, lass. You'd be cranky, too." Valerian answers as he steps into the room. He winks at her.

She cocks an eyebrow at Daire and Astor.

"One thousand six hundred and forty-five, gorgeous. I'm in my prime." Astor wriggles his eyebrows as he replies.

Daire sighs. "One thousand six hundred and three."

"Ah, so you're the baby," she teases him.

He scowls at her in return.

Interrupting the age discussion, I fill them in on my conversation with Cormal. "It's unusual. Cormal has never let me down. The fact he can't find a good lead means we're looking at royalty. Which means this became a hundred times harder. Why don't we start at the beginning? Arden, can you walk us through the attempts so far?"

Pacing, her long legs eat up the room while she lists out the facts. "The first known assassination attempt killed my mother. She'd left to meet my father, but we don't know if he showed or not. Solandis went to the meeting spot a couple of days later and found her dead, a Killian blade in her heart."

"Where did she find her?" I interrupt.

"In a hut on the edge of the Wilds, between the Elven and Fae territories," she replies. "Solandis believes my mom died shortly before she got there, because she found her body still warm. She didn't see, smell, or feel anyone, though."

"The Wilds, huh? I'll have Cormal check out the hut. Can you ask Solandis to send me the coordinates?" I ask.

She nods and continues, "The other attempts have been random. For most of my life, I've lived in a pocket dimension with Solandis, Vargas, and Callyx. I rarely left, but when I did, they only allowed me to visit the land of the Fae or the Underworld. And yet, the assassins always found me. We fended off fourteen additional attempts during those visits, which brings the total to fifteen. The sixteenth attempt happened before I came here. They found our home. Solandis and I killed them, but the third Killian blade came with them. My mother left instructions for me to find Theron when the third blade appeared. I came here the next day. Today was the seventeenth attempt."

Several questions pop into my head. "Besides the Killian blades, did they have any special weapons on them?"

Arden thinks about it for a second. "The usual magical assortment, but nothing special."

"Can you tell me anything about the attackers?" I probe.

"They seem to be from all races. Fae, demons, shifters, vampires, warlocks, trolls, witches," she says, listing them off.

Straightening, I pick up on a lead. "What about elves?"

Arden closes her eyes to bring up the details of each attack. "No elves. Ever. That's kind of weird, right?"

"Yes, it's strange. But it might be an advantage for us," I muse. "My reach and contacts are strongest in the Elven realm. My father's, too."

"I don't want your father to know about Arden," Theron interjects. "It's too dangerous. If he's a part of the problem, it could backfire on us."

"I highly doubt my father has a contract out on Arden," I argue. "He could be a big help."

"No," Theron replies.

"I agree with Theron," Valerian states.

"Astor? Daire?" I say, asking for their opinion.

"We might need his contacts. Maybe you can ask without alerting him to the fact Arden is here with us? Make it seem as if Cormal made an inquiry, and you're suspicious about anything Cormal wants to know," Daire suggests.

"Sounds like an excellent compromise," states Astor. "We get his input without showing our hand."

I agree. "Theron? Valerian? What do you think?"

"That works," Valerian says gruffly.

Theron stares at me, silently telling me not to fuck this up. "I agree."

"And if anyone cares what I think..." Arden glares at all of us before continuing, "I agree, too. But nothing remains a secret in court, so the fewer people who know my situation, the better."

"After this discussion, I'll reach out to my father and Cormal. I don't want Cormal blindsided if my father calls on him." I push the hair back from my face. "I've got one more question. If we think these assassination attempts relate to your father, we need to figure out who he is sooner rather than later. Do you have any ideas? Any unusual powers?"

"Well, I can read minds. Is that a witch power?" Arden says, peering at Astor and Daire for their input. We all stop what we're doing to stare at Arden.

Shocked, I try to empty my mind of thoughts, but new thoughts keep pouring in like sand in an hourglass. Looking around the room, I notice the panic on Valerian's face, and the ice frosting the wall behind Theron. Daire and Astor are the only ones who aren't panicking. Instead, they just seem amused.

"Just kidding." Arden laughs. "Although, looking at your faces, I wish I had the power." She sighs. "So far, I've only been able to use my witch powers. But as I've learned this week, sometimes you have to know how to use a power. I didn't know I could transfigure until today. Once Santiago walked me through it, I knew I could do it. Can I practice with some of you?" She blinks at Astor. "Not blood magic. Think I'll wait to try that one again. But demon magic? Fae magic? Elven magic? I don't know. Thoughts?"

"It's worth a try. We'll take turns with you and see if anything resonates," Theron remarks.

Arden raises her finger. "But first, this week, I need to learn how to heal. Daire is going to teach me the way his mother taught him. I know I can pass all six bloodline tests, but I don't want Caro to know until the placement ceremony."

"Don't they usually finish the testing prior to the ceremony?" I ask her.

"I believe so. Santiago is going to suggest we hold both the tests and the ceremony at the same time," she explains.

"Good. That gives us a few more days to prepare for it." I sigh and roll my neck. "I'll go call my father. Theron, do you want to go with me to make sure I don't inadvertently give him any clues?" Knowing his need for control, I offer him an olive branch.

With a nod, he shifts his gaze to Arden. "From now on, you will take one of us with you when you leave. More than one might be better. This is non-negotiable," he demands.

Arden stares him down but says nothing.

He gestures for me to wait. "Promise me."

Arden crosses her arms and promises, "I promise to always take someone with me."

I interject, "One of the cadre. At least until we can figure out who's behind the assassination attempts."

She blows out a breath. "Fine. I agree to take one of the cadre."

23

ARDEN

As I'm drying myself off, I hear a knock on my bedroom door. A quick twist secures the towel around me, and I pull it open to find Theron.

"Why do I always find you half-dressed?" Theron mutters.

"Maybe it's the only way I can get your attention?" I reply, half joking.

Theron ignores the statement. "I came by to inform you the call with the light Elven king went well. He's going to have his chief of security investigate the contract. Although, I can't say for certain he'll tell us everything he finds. Time will tell."

My stomach tightens. "I guess one more person helping isn't a bad thing, but for some reason, it doesn't feel all that great, either."

Theron nods absentmindedly as he gazes around the room. "It's taking on your personality."

Startled, I look around. The Killian blades hang on the wall, along with a few more weapons. My family grimoire lies on the desk, open to a spell I was practicing before bed last night. A picture of Solandis, Vargas, me, and Callyx sits on the nightstand. "I guess I feel comfortable here," I say self-consciously. Startled, I realize it's true. The Abbey feels like home.

"Good. We want you to feel comfortable here," he murmurs. "Also, Reyna is downstairs. Do you want me to escort her up?"

Frowning, I wonder what she could want, but I doubt it's anything I want the rest of the club staff to overhear. "Yes, please send her up. I need to dry my hair and get dressed."

He nods, then strides closer to me, backing me into the door. "Before I leave, I need to clear up this little misunderstanding between us."

"Misunderstanding?" I ask, frowning.

He sweeps an icy finger down my cheek, causing me to shiver. "You always have my attention. Whether you're working, training with Valerian and Astor, bending back the finger of an incubus who's clearly overstepped his bounds, threatening Amelie, or manipulating Caro, I see you." Theron picks up my hand. "When you're not in sight, I wonder what you're doing, and sometimes I worry. When I organize my day, I make sure it includes an excuse to see you. Attention? I wouldn't worry about something so mundane. You captured my attention the first night you came here." He strokes a hand over my head, then shifts me to the side of the door. I blink, and he's gone.

I guess that's what happens when you push an arrogant Fae's buttons. I smile, determined to do it more often. He needs to let loose. I groan as I picture all that control flying out the window, and let's just say I desperately want it.

With a sigh, I run my hand over my hair and realize it's dry. Theron must have dried it when he had me up against the door. I quickly dress, finishing just as another knock sounds on the door.

When I open the door this time, Reyna stands on the other

side. I step back and leave the door open. While I don't consider us enemies, we're not friends, either.

"Hello, Reyna. This is a surprise. How's Santiago doing after last night's battle?" I ask, motioning for her to step into the room.

She scans the room, eyes trailing from my grimoire on the desk to the weapons on the wall. "He's sore, but with a few potions, he's healing fast. I'm surprised to see you up, though. Based on the description he gave me of your wounds, I expected you to be down for a week, at least." Suspicion rings in her voice. "He sent me here to check on you. See if you had enough potions."

"Hmm…Astor makes remarkable potions," I answer vaguely. "And thank you for checking on me. I'm actually on my way out to meet Cassandra. You're welcome to come."

She snorts. "No, an afternoon shopping with Cassandra and her posse is at the top of my never fucking ever list, but thanks. I'll let my father know how well you're doing." Reyna pauses. "Word of advice? Cassandra is worse than Caro. At least Caro cares about the good of the coven. Cassandra? She only cares about Cassandra. Don't trust her."

BEFORE I MEET WITH CASSANDRA, I STOP BY ASTOR'S ROOM. When I don't find him there, I text Theron, who keeps tabs on all of us. Theron gives me directions to Astor's lab, and orders me to remind Astor that he needs to eat and sleep. Apparently, he spends a lot of time in the lab experimenting with spells and potions. Who knew my favorite warlock was a magical nerd? Of course, he's the only warlock I know, but it's kind of sexy when I think about it.

The door is open when I get to the lab, and I find Astor pouring liquid from one beaker to the other. Standing silently in the doorway, I watch him. His face is serious and full of concentration as he carefully mixes the two liquids. Once the left beaker is full, he swirls the liquid, turning it from lime green to a stunning purple. He sets the full beaker on the stand in front of him and places the empty beaker in a nearby sink.

"Wow, the sexy incubus is actually a bona fide nerd," I tease, walking quietly into the room. "Don't worry, I won't tell anyone. Your reputation would only benefit, and you have a big enough head already."

Startled, Astor whips around and grabs my hand. "Gorgeous!" He lifts it to place a kiss on the inside of my wrist. "So, you think nerds are sexy, huh? Should I put on a pair of glasses and a white coat? We could role play. You know, I could be the mad scientist and you could be my research assistant. We could experiment together."

I laugh loudly at his antics. "Hmm...as tempting as that sounds, I need to be somewhere in twenty minutes. I came here to ask you for a favor," I tell him. Though, I am tempted to stay and play with this Astor. Who knew Astor could shed the intensely sexual incubus role for this more playful and nerdier one?

His smile dims with my response. "What can I do for you?"

"When we were at Amelie's house, I noticed you had a truth rune tattooed on your arm. Is this something you could tattoo on me?" I bite my lip, waiting for his response.

His eyes are serious as he weighs my request. "I could, but I wouldn't do that to you. Speaking from experience, it's the most brutal rune on my body. People lie all the time. Little lies, big lies. Feeling the rune flare every time someone lies shreds any faith you have in them. It's like dying from a thousand paper cuts. But when the lie comes from the closest of friends or lovers, it cuts to the bone, shattering your love for them. If I had to do it all over again, knowing what I know now, I wouldn't do it. I can't grant this favor. I'm sorry, gorgeous." His eyes beseech me to understand the cruelty of my request.

I can't help it, I hug him tightly. "I understand. I only wanted to use it as an advantage on my enemies, not as a weapon for my friends and family. Whether I'm using it on them or they're inadvertently using it on me, I refuse to sacrifice those relationships." I sweep his auburn hair back from his face. "And now that I know how you feel about the rune, I'll try to make sure I lie to you every day."

"Why would you lie to me?"

I smirk. "Because you like a little pain. Don't worry. They'll be little white lies. Small, tiny stings designed to make your blood sing."

His eyes light up in delight. "Hmm, kinky. I like it. Now kiss me before you leave."

I tease him with a kiss on the corner of his mouth. "Make sure you eat and drink something today. See you later, my mad scientist."

"MY MOTHER TELLS ME YOU'RE COMPLETING THE FINAL TWO bloodline tests on the same day and holding your placement ceremony immediately afterwards," Cassandra remarks. Tilting her head to the side, she considers me.

My face blank, I blandly reply, "Really? Nobody's mentioned it to me."

"My mother is impatient to find out your bloodlines so she can finish tracing your lineage back to your parents," she informs me. "I'm not sure why she's waiting. The Martinez family has withheld bloodline six from the coven for years. And I doubt you're a descendant of the Lee family, like me."

Lifting my hands, I imply a lack of interest. "I consider my guardians my parents. What does it matter who my real parents were?"

"It's important for us to record every single witch. Our numbers and powers are minimal compared to past witches. My mother is researching to find the reason and a solution. Having your background information is important for the coven's future." She recites this information as if she's heard it a million times.

"I'm learning more about us each day," I murmur as a dress in the window catches my eye. Made of amber silk, with a halter neck and a long slit up the side, it screams sexy sophistication, and the color reminds me of Valerian's eyes. "I'm going to try on that dress." I step into the store.

An older lady approaches me. "Can I help you find something?"

Her name tag says "Anna." "Hello, Anna. I'd like to try on the dress in the window, please. Do you have it in a size six?"

She glances down and gives me a fake smile. "Absolutely. I'll get it for you."

"Thank you." I look around to see if there's anything else. Amelie destroyed my clothes, so I need quite a bit, and several items catch my eye. Cassandra stands in the shop's entrance. "The clothes here are fabulous. Good quality, interesting designs. Have you shopped here?"

Her nose wrinkles in distaste. "I like my clothes much more form-fitting," she scoffs, waving a hand at her ripped skinny jeans and skin-tight crop top, then laughs loudly.

I shrug. "I like classic lines," I state, ignoring her last statement. Anna steps out from the back with the amber dress. "Wonderful. I'll also try on these three shirts, two pairs of pants and this moto jacket."

Anna frowns, but turns and walks back to the dressing rooms.

"I'll be right back. We could meet at the food court?" I offer.

"I'm good," she replies with a giggle, then whispers something to the rest of the group.

The clothes fit beautifully, including the moto jacket. I pile the items on the counter and wait for Anna to ring me up.

Anna wraps them up and states the total.

I hand her my card, then turn to Cassandra and the rest of the group. "Thanks for waiting. Let's go grab something to eat."

When we step out of the store, Essa blurts, "I like the dress you bought."

Cassandra glares at her.

I guess Cassandra doesn't like it when her minions have their own opinions.

We all grab something to eat and sit down in the middle of the food court. Cassandra and her posse on one side of the table, with myself on the other.

"So, Cassandra, can you tell me anything about the placement ceremony?" I say nonchalantly.

"God, I forget how ignorant you are about witch stuff. First, they read the results from your bloodline tests to the entire coven. I guess in your case, they'll finish the last two tests before they read the results. You place your hand on the witches' thorn, and it decides your acceptance into the coven. Then, Caro decides on your placement in the hierarchy and how you will help support the coven. Kind of like the job you'll do for the coven. They inform you and your family. Finally, you give your blood oath to the coven. That's it."

I'd heard some of this from Bianca, but not the last part. "I thought witches didn't work? And what's a witches' thorn?" I ask, then take a bite of my pizza. "Also, can I invite my family to the placement ceremony?"

She sighs, as if my questions are taxing her. "First, you take on jobs for the coven. If Caro needs you to research something, she gives you a job, but it's not like a job outside of the coven. Second, it's a thorn, from our sacred rowan tree. When you place your hand down on it, your blood mingles with the blood of all the other witches before you. Magic tied to the thorn reveals where you should be placed on the family tree," Cassandra states, her tone matter of fact.

I don't like the idea of them having a drop of my blood. As I experienced when I used blood magic, it's pure power. "You carve my name into a tree?" I ask, puzzled.

I think it's Essa who replies while giggling. "No, silly. The coven's family tree is a tapestry of the sacred rowan. The magic weaves every witch's name onto the tree."

Interesting. "Every witch? Even those born as a hybrid, like Daire and Astor?" I drill, already guessing the answer.

"Of course not. Only pure witches may put their name on the tree. We don't consider hybrids witches," sneers Cassandra.

"Pure witches, got it. Anything else?" I murmur, trying to control my anger.

"Well, there's your allegiance to the light," Cassandra laughs, "or the dark. Obviously, the light has all the power in our coven, so if you want to pick the winning side, you'll choose light. It represents the greater good of the coven. We all want what's best for the coven, right?"

"I don't think free will is so bad," I state firmly, referencing the dark. After all, I grew up in a house with both light and dark.

"Maybe not in other races, but for witches, the dark has little power," she says. Cassandra stands and tosses her hair. "And of course, you can bring your family. My mother is looking forward to meeting them and hearing your history. Well, we've got to go. See you in a few days." With the two other witches, she walks out of the food court, leaving me to digest all the information she let slip.

Valerian waits until they're completely out of sight, then walks over to me. "Did you get any new information?"

I wrap my hand around his arm. "I did. And I found out I'm

allowed to invite my family to the ceremony. Would you like to go?"

He stares down at me, emotions swirling in his eyes, "Lass, I don't think they'll let you bring me."

"Why? I'm adopted," I remind him. "In my life, I've had to adopt my family. I choose to adopt you and the rest of the cadre. Besides, it's not like Theron is going to stay at home and let me go to the placement ceremony by myself."

He snorts. "Not only Theron. We'll talk it over and decide who's going to go. Now, are you ready?"

Shaking my bags, I nod. "Ready. And I've found the perfect dress for the ceremony. Matches your eyes."

He stills, stares down at my lips and mutters, "We need to have a talk soon, lass."

24

ARDEN

Theron is standing by the elevator when Valerian drops me off. At least this time, I'm fully dressed. I glance up and find him staring down at me, but he says nothing. What's he thinking about? Probably something utterly mundane, like his schedule. Although, wouldn't it be wonderful if I was wrong? From what he said earlier, he thinks about me more than I imagined. He certainly intrigues me. He's everywhere, taking care of the cadre, me, The Abbey, and his Fae duties. We would all fail if Theron wasn't around.

I clear my throat and step into the elevator, where I'm trapped. The smell of dark chocolate and peppermint fills the air, making me...hungry. He murmurs something, but I miss it. "I'm sorry, what did you say?"

"I instructed the elevator to stop at your room first," he informs me. "Are you okay?"

"Yes," I reply. Silence reigns in the elevator, so I blurt out, "Can I borrow the book in your office?"

He tilts his head. "What book?"

Thinking back to the titles on the shelves, I reply, "I think it's called *The Harmony of Technology and Magic?*"

He stares at me, trying to decipher the meaning behind my request. "I'll drop it off later."

The elevator opens. Thank the fuck. "Thanks, I appreciate it," I call out, launching through the door of my room like a rocket and falling on my bed facedown. "I'm such a fucking idiot." The man makes me nervous, with his violet eyes and effortless perfection, and I find myself wanting to please him just so I can see his almost imperceptible reactions. Those tiny tells shout louder than any words.

I CLOSE THE BOOK ON THE FOUNDING WITCH FAMILIES. MY MIND is racing with all the pieces of the puzzle, turning them, trying to find the right fit. I'm close. I can feel it. Without this book, it would have taken me a lot longer to figure things out, and it's all thanks to Meri.

With a pause, I consider that statement. *How did Meri know I needed this book?*

My hand reaches for my phone, and I send her a quick text to ask if she wants to go out this evening for a girls' night. I haven't seen much of the city, and I've been promising her I'd go out for a week, at least. She replies quickly with a place and time, giving me thirty minutes to get ready. I shoot off another text and jump up to get ready.

With a couple of spells, I arrange my hair into a half up, half down style, then enhance my makeup with smokier eyes and plump lips. I check the mirror, nod at the results, then walk over to the closet. This is going to be the tough part. While a witch can conjure clothes, we typically don't. Any interference with our magic, and we'd be standing naked. I shudder. *No, thank you.*

Flicking through the sparse choices, I settle on an off the shoulder sweater in green that makes my eyes pop, black skinny jeans, and black booties. This seems nice enough to go to dinner or a club, depending on where the mood takes us. After a spritz of perfume and grabbing my clutch, I'm sailing through the door and into the elevator, straight into Theron's arms—strong arms that immediately wrap around me.

What are the fucking odds?

I pull back and cringe. "Sorry, Theron. I'm in a hurry to meet Meri, and I didn't see you. Lobby, please. Oh, the book. Thank you. Would you mind putting it in my room? Thanks. I'll see you later." The doors open, and I jump out of the elevator before I make a bigger fool of myself.

"Wait," Theron demands. "Who's going with you?"

"I am," Astor drawls, stepping from the shadows.

Theron gives me a satisfied nod and Astor an intense stare, probably ordering him to not let me out of his sight.

Astor laughs and tells Theron, "Stop worrying, old man. We're going to have some fun."

Meri is standing to the side watching, so I grab her arm and hurry out the door. "Astor is coming with us tonight, huh?" She winks at me.

I glance back. Astor leisurely follows behind us, close enough to protect but, thankfully, far enough away to give us some privacy to chat. I groan and shove her. "Stop. He's my bodyguard."

"Right," she agrees. "An incubus guarding your body. Isn't that a bit like the fox guarding the henhouse?"

"First, he's more than an incubus. He's a warlock," I say exasperatedly. "And second, I'm one of many his incubus wants."

Meri shakes her head, disagreeing with me. "I wouldn't be so sure. He's different around you, like he sees only you. There's an intensity to how he feels. Don't push him away. You'll regret it."

"Are you using your seer power?" I tease her.

"I wasn't using your seer power, just my own two eyes," she laughingly protests.

"*My* seer power? I don't have any seer power. Believe me, if I did, I'd be using it all the time right now," I assure her.

Meri grabs my arm and pulls me closer to whisper in my ear. "Actually, you do. *I* don't have seer power. I used your power the other night." She glances around to make sure nobody is near. "I'm a mimic. I pick up and use others' powers. Not all the time, and I can't use everyone's powers, but at least half of the time."

Shocked, I'm not sure where to start first—my seer power or her ability to mimic. "Is that how you knew I needed the book on witches and the founding families?" I ask, starting with my fundamental question from earlier.

"Yes. I saw you reading the book, and I knew. I'd seen it in a library, so I pulled it for you," she replies. "I know you want to see the future, but your seer ability is bound, along with your other powers. As one returns, so will the others."

I blow out the breath I'm holding. Having my mother's power means something to me, not just because it would help me find my way but because it's something we could share. But apparently, not today. Nothing happens until destiny wills it. I want to scream with frustration, but I don't want to upset Meri. Wait… "Oooh, can you use those other powers, the powers from my father?"

"No. They're blocked for some reason. I can see this ball of power, but I can't access it. It's as if a net contains them," she replies. "I'm sorry."

Disappointed, I blow out a breath. "It's fine. Just trying to figure out a few things. And thank you. The book has been extremely helpful. So, do you have other magic besides your ability to mimic?"

She shakes her head. "Sadly, no. I'm a sitting duck until I can pick up someone else's powers. Please, please don't tell anyone. My adopted mother would be furious, but I wanted you to know. Any time you feel my power, it's actually coming from someone else. When we met, you thought I was powerful, but you were actually picking up on your power, I was only mimicking. It's why I enjoy working at The Abbey, because it's easy to pick up and use others' magic. It doesn't hurt them, and the power never leaves them for me."

I nod, staring down at her. That's a pretty big secret. I've never even heard of a mimic in our world. "We're friends. Your secret is safe with me."

"Friends," she says, smiling. "I know we share a destiny because I saw our fate linked in my first vision. Sadly, I didn't get any details. But friendship, I didn't see that coming. I've never had a friend." She laughs and swings an arm around me. "Now, let's go get something to drink and eat. Maybe dance. Not at The Abbey. Somewhere new and wonderful." She's bouncing with joy and energy as she drags me down the street.

25

ARDEN

After Astor buys us dinner, he drags us to a dance club called Devil's Lair. While all supernaturals are welcome, he explains it's mainly a hangout for denizens of the Underworld —demons, incubi, warlocks, hellhounds, and the like. Astor ignores the line and walks right up to the massive troll guarding the door, who immediately bows to Astor, runs his eyes over us, and then waves his hand to let us in the club.

With a deep voice, he says, "Have a good evening."

Meri grabs my hand. "Are you sure about this place?"

"It can't be much different than the place Callyx took me to in the Underworld. Underworld races are massively territorial and possessive. If you're with someone, they usually won't bother you. And who's going to mess with Astor?" I motion to the crowd parting before us.

She relaxes. "You're right. Only the criminally stupid would mess with him and the cadre." With a laugh, she twirls in a circle. "Let's have some fun!"

Several handsome men turn to watch Meri dance around me. "The eye candy in this place is sublime. And they all look like they want to devour you," I murmur to her.

Meri glances to the side. "I'm not the only one they're watching."

Astor suddenly appears, wraps a hand around my waist, and leans in to whisper in my ear, "You can look, but don't even think about touching. The only person you're going home with tonight is me." His dark brown eyes are fierce as he frowns at the crowd.

"You don't own me," I furiously whisper back.

"No, but I'm thinking you own us." He gives a husky chuckle as he lifts a hand, and a hostess comes over. "We'd like a VIP booth, please."

She slides her eyes over him and flushes. "Right this way, sir." She strolls over to the stairs and takes us to the second floor, where she points to a deep purple velvet couch with a coffee table in front of it. "Will this do?"

Astor glances down, inclines his head, and hands her some money. "Thank you, this works. Send over the server."

The hostess slides her hand over Astor's, lingers for a second, then takes the money. She whispers her thanks and slides him a piece of paper.

Rolling my eyes, I pull Meri down on the couch with me. "See what I mean?"

"What? Sorry, I was admiring the...scenery." With a lick of her lips, she leans back so I can see the table of sexy, tattooed men sitting next to us. "I need to get out more."

Astor sits on my other side. He follows our eyes to the table next to us. "Mmm...I agree. There's enough sexual testosterone in that group to dine for days." He moves restlessly beside me.

"You don't have to stick this close to me. If you want to visit with them, go. When I want to dance, I'll let you know," I tell him, although it takes everything in me to say it. I know he's an incubus and needs sex for sustenance and power, but a part of me hates the idea.

Deep brown eyes gaze down at me—Astor, but not Astor. "Liar. You don't want me to go," he marvels, and a seductive smile slides onto his face.

I huff. "I said…"

He chuckles. "I know what you desire, even when you don't say it, and you desire us."

I glance over at Meri, who's listening. She mouths, "I told you so." I glare at her and tap the button on the table to call the server. Seconds later, a mouthwatering male wearing black pants and a bow tie with washboard abs comes to our table. My body tingles, and my nipples harden. Breathing deeply, I moan, but the rune at my throat flares in warning.

A deep chuckle from Astor brings me out of my semi-trance. "Do you like what you see, gorgeous?"

"What the hell?" I stand, fists clenched. "What are you trying to pull?"

The server stares at Astor and states, "Not your usual?"

Astor gives him a wry smile. "Not tonight. Sorry, I forgot to warn you. We'll have a bottle of champagne, please."

He dips his chin and heads off to get a bottle.

Meri glares at me and Astor. "Well, hell. I'm all hot and bothered now. I'm going to dance. You two stay here and figure this out." She jumps up and heads downstairs to the dance floor, then several guys from the table beside us follow her.

I take a step to go after her, and Astor stops me.

"She'll be fine. I'll keep an eye on her," Astor assures me. "And I'm sorry. Lucas, our server, is a lust demon. When I've brought dates here in the past, he's amped up the atmosphere, and as a reward, I've invited him to join the party." He looks up, his gaze lingering on my hard nipples, before drifting up to my eyes. "Please sit back down."

I swallow. "Maybe I should go dance with Meri." I scan around for her silver hair. The dance floor is packed, but I finally spot her, dancing, sandwiched between two guys. I snort. She'd kill me if I interrupted her now.

Astor stands, pulling my back to his front. "You should let her have some fun. Stay here with me. Please." His lips trail down my neck to caress the shoulder left bare by my sweater.

A little of his power slips, and I moan, then with a simple turn, my body lines up with every delicious inch of his. I stare at his throat, trying desperately to hold on to my sanity.

Could I do this? Could I let loose?

His fingers grasp my chin, and he pulls it up, waiting until my eyes meet his. This time, his incubus stares back. His normally deep brown eyes are practically black, desire making them gleam like obsidian. A carnal smile graces his firm lips. "Stop thinking and feel. Let the desire fill you up. When you're on the edge, ready to fly, kiss me," he instructs, his voice deep while his power slides over me, caressing me, as if it's alive. "That's it. Just a kiss."

I sigh. Astor is temptation and pure sin wrapped up in a luscious package. In over three hundred years, I'd only been with a few males, mostly Fae and mostly strangers, someone to satisfy an itch but not anyone worthy of note. They were rushed affairs lasting a night or, at most, a few weeks. Between the constant isolation and the assassination attempts, the opportunity to let go never presented itself, until tonight. My body strains toward his, demanding he follow through.

One hand remains on my waist, while the other cups my head. To the patrons in the club, we're locked into a staring match, not moving, but beneath the illusion, his power, a whisper and a shadow, is everywhere. It seeps into my skin, amplifying my desire, seeking those secret places only lovers know. As it flicks and licks, I bite my lip to hold in my moans.

It's relentless in the pursuit of my pleasure. His power dips down between my legs, and I try to clamp them together, but nothing can prevent it from finding its treasure. With the first lick of my clit, I gasp and grab Astor, my hand fisting in his shirt. With sly little flicks and sucks, it brings me to the edge and then stops, over and over again, until I'm permanently on the edge, standing there waiting to fly. Desperate for relief, I whimper.

What did he say? That's right—a kiss. Just one kiss.

My mouth latches on to his, pouring my desire into him, wanting him to know the depth of my need, to feel it. It knows no boundaries. All the time I've spent alone is a blip in time compared to this moment. Every second of waiting was worth it as I kiss and kiss and kiss. Leaving sanity and air behind, I can't kiss him deeply enough. I'm fulfilled, wanting nothing more than to kiss him. Until he kisses me back.

At first, his kiss is sensual, savoring my lips, nibbling here and there, before lightly sucking my bottom lip, teasing me, tempting me. I moan, and it's the song he's been waiting to hear, driving him to deepen the kiss until he's devouring me. It's never-ending. He groans and digs his fingers into my hair, taking what I give him and returning it tenfold. Power and magic swirl around us, in us, magnifying our desire until I soar over the edge. His lips capture my deep moan, keeping it secretly between us.

Breathing heavily, I pull away from his lips, stunned to find myself fully clothed and still standing in the middle of our VIP section, my lips and body thrumming with satiated pleasure. "What...How did you do that?" I ask huskily.

"I combined our magic. Physically, my incubus can use shadows to caress and stroke you without being seen. Combined with the power you shared with me the other day, I created a scenario for us to see and experience in our minds. Our desire did the rest," he rasps. "And damn, it was incredible, more than I imagined. Your desire and ours together tore the floor out from under me. I want to take you home and lock you in my room for weeks." He stares down at me with flushed cheeks, desire riding him hard.

"I…" My phone dings with a text. It's Meri. I look down on the dance floor and see her waving at me.

MERI: I'M HEADING OUT. YOU OKAY?

Arden: I'm fine. Are you going home with someone? Take a picture and send it to me. You know, in case I need to rescue you.

Meri: Here. Don't rescue me too soon.

A picture of the two guys I saw her dancing with earlier shows up on my screen. *Two?!*

Arden: Mmm, hot. Be safe. I'll see you at work tomorrow night.

Meri: xxx

"MERI IS LEAVING. I'D LIKE TO GET OUT OF HERE, TOO," I TELL Astor. "Do you mind?"

With a sinful smile, he replies, "Hell no. Let's go."

We catch a car back to The Abbey, where Astor picks up a bottle of champagne from the bar. The elevator drops us off at his room, but I hesitate.

He sweeps my hair back and smiles softly. "Just a kiss, remember?"

Remembering our terms, I follow him into his bedroom and shut the door behind us.

26

ARDEN

After spending the night with Astor, I feel incredible. We spent the entire night kissing and using our shared power, but we never had sex. He pushed my limits, teasing me with his magic until I was begging for release, but his incubus seemed to be content with the foreplay. I sigh. If this is just the foreplay stage, I'm not sure I'll survive having sex with him.

We talked a lot, too, about magic, mostly—our best and worst magic. Astor understands what it feels like to be powerful and alone, relying only on yourself and books to help you learn.

Solandis brought in a few tutors for me, but we were in hiding. She had to be careful with who she picked, so the more powerful I became, the fewer tutors we brought into our bubble.

Astor's father taught him about his incubus powers, but the witch and blood magic had to be learned on his own. While we didn't talk about his past, I don't think his mother was around much.

With a yawn, I text Meri to make sure she made it home.

She replies with a picture of a bed, two hard bodies, and the words "Not yet."

Grinning, I tell her I'll see her at work tonight.

Changing into my workout clothes, I head towards the gym. Valerian is waiting to wipe the floor with me, and I can't disappoint the man.

"Lass, distraction is a dirty tactic, almost as dirty as a punch to the balls," he growls. He eyes my tiny shorts and long legs, then heaves a sigh. "Fair's fair." He grabs the back of his shirt and pulls it off. "Now, can we get down to battle?"

I choke on my water. That damn dragon should never wear clothes. Every muscle is a lesson in anatomy, hard with grooves and lines exactly where they should be, a perfect specimen. With a grin, I decide to tease him a little more. "Almost, let me put down this water bottle." I slowly bend down and place the bottle on the floor.

I'm not even fully standing before he's charging. My shield drops into place, and I run up the wall, until I flip, landing behind him.

He turns, a long mace in his hand, and I duck. A quick spell turns the mace into a snake, until fire runs down his arm incinerating the snake.

On and on, I throw spells, and he counters. He attacks, I parry. Fire, ice, and shadows pour out of him, and I defuse each power, one after the other.

Our breaths are harsh, grunts and whistles filling the air, and I'm a sweaty, heaving mess. Running my arm across my forehead, I try to wipe off the sweat rushing towards my eyes, and that's when he pounces.

Swiping my legs out from under me, I go down hard, but not without catching his ankle first. He hurtles toward me, dropping like a stone directly on top of me. With a *whoosh*, my breath spills out of my lungs.

Valerian immediately eases his weight off me, but I'm unable to breathe. He jerks me toward him and gives me the air from his lungs. Over and over, he breathes air into me and my lungs until I'm able to take a breath, then another.

Placing my hand on his shoulder, I cough and suck in as much air as I can get. I breathe in deeply over and over until I'm breathing normally again. "You weigh a ton."

His voice is full of Scotland and tartans when he answers. "Lass, I'm a full-grown dragon. What do ya expect?" His accent is thick with concern as his fingers trail over my face, mapping each feature.

"Thank you for being the air I breathe," I murmur, my eyes falling to his firm lips. After spending the night kissing Astor, all I can think about is kissing, kissing, and more kissing. Add in a half-naked dragon, all muscles and sweetness, and I'm a goner. I reach up to pull him down to me, and he freezes.

"Lass, I really, really want to kiss you, but I can't," he groans. "I've got something to tell you, and I've been trying to figure out a way to say it."

Anxiety fills me, making my stomach cramp. I sit up, pushing him back so I can see his face. "Tell me," I demand.

He goes into a long explanation of the reasons the dragons use the chamber—crowning king, presenting your mate, and death. Got it. "It's a vision. It might not even be real. And I saw you, you're not dead."

"It's blood magic, and while it can deceive, it can't lie. If we're in the king's chamber and I'm alive, then the only other reason is to present my mate to my clan," he explains.

My mind whirls, trying to remember the details of the vision. The dragons yelling, "Kill the witch", Valerian arguing with those two men, and the stabbing. "You think I'm your mate?" I whisper. Emotions swirl in my head and heart. Every supernatural wants to find their mate or mates. Happiness fills me, then dread. The timing isn't ideal. I mean, assassins attacked me just the other day. "Really?"

"Unfortunately, yes," he replies.

Unfortunately? What the hell? I think, ignoring the fact I was just pondering the same thing.

Tears rise, but I push them down and tuck them away, letting anger replace them. I demand, "Unfortunately? I mean, I know we're just getting to know each other and I'm not an expert on being someone's mate, but I don't think that's the best way to tell them. It's supposed to be happy, isn't it? Does this feel happy to you?"

He grabs my hands. "Will you let me finish?" he roars impatiently. "Of course I want you, lass. But I need to explain something." He pauses, then blurts out, "My clan won't accept a witch for a mate."

I frown, reading the truth in his eyes. "Are you saying you need the permission of your clan?"

He snorts. "That day will never come. Because of what happened in the past, they've never forgiven the witches, or me," he reflects. "I'm not sure what they'll do. They might try to kill you, or kill me. I'm not sure I can protect you against my entire clan if they're out for blood. I can abdicate, but what if I can't protect you because I don't have the power of a king anymore?"

I listen to what he's saying and what he's not, then I laugh. "And I was worried about my assassins killing you. What's this world coming to when you can't mate because death threats are on the table? But then again, mating is never easy. I mean, look at Solandis and Vargas. They were the first Fae and demon mating. Their pairing almost started a war.

"Here's the deal—few are lucky enough to be given a mate. If the fates paired us, I have to believe there's a way to get past your clan, my assassins, and whatever destiny has in store for us," I tell him. When he tries to interrupt, I brush my finger across his lips to silence him. "I think the biggest issue is your past. You're scared the past will repeat itself, and I get it. Your entire life crashed down on you because you loved a witch." I pull my hand from his mouth and cup his cheek. "I know you say you want me, but do you want a mate? A mate means giving me something bigger than your heart. It's binding your soul to mine for eternity. Losing Moira hurt you deeply. Take some time and think about it, but for every day you make me wait, I'll torture you when you finally cave."

He stands and pulls me up beside him. "Lass, I don't need time to think about it. I loved Moira, truly, but she passed a long time ago. I've been alone for over a thousand years and never thought twice about it. Then you come along and shock the hell out of me. Here's this beautiful, powerful warrior, fighting her own battles and searching for her destiny. You're a hell of a wake-up call." He chuckles, then takes a deep breath. "But I want you to think about it. I can't guarantee your safety or the acceptance of my clan. If I abdicate, I can't offer you the position as queen by my side. The only thing I have to offer is myself, and that's not much."

I start to protest. "I don't have to think about it—"

He places a finger on my lips. "Please. Just give it a week or two. I want you to really think about it."

Frustrated, I blow out a breath. I completely disagree, but I can see the worry on his face. "Fine."

He wraps his massive arms around me and gives me a hug, and I smile. My mate is a dragon, and not just any dragon, but a dragon of legends. Vargas is going to be so proud.

27

DAIRE

I watch Arden weave in and out of the tables below. With her hair flowing behind her, she's like a warrior out for someone's blood in her tight black tank top, miniskirt, and boots. Her expression is fierce and brooding as she approaches her tables, then it's as if a switch is flipped and she's all smiles, flirting with the males and flashing skin wherever she goes.

Valerian mutters behind me. His whiskey is gripped tightly in his hand while his eyes follow Arden's every move. I laugh at the misery on his face. Clearly, Arden's show is for him, and it's working.

Astor, Fallon, and Theron arrive minutes later, and the crowd goes silent. It's the first time we've stood together in the VIP section in years. I wave my hand, motioning for them to continue doing whatever they were doing.

My back to the railing, I watch the cadre. Theron has got his nose buried deep in his phone, but he occasionally looks up to check on Arden. Astor is rubbing his fingers across his lips and smiling. His dark eyes gleam as he follows Arden, not even noticing the busty brunette that's been eyeing him for ten minutes. Fallon is scanning the crowd, as if he expects an assassin at any minute, his stance light and ready to intervene. All of this is because of Arden. She's changing us, taking our loose threads and weaving them tighter together.

Even I'm not immune. She's brought light back into my life, a life that's been cold and dark since Danica died. When I healed Arden the other day, it was as if my heart beat again. While my heart can beat, it's unnecessary, so I suppress it, because it's a reminder of my humanity and I'd rather embrace my true predatory nature.

I sip my drink and turn to watch the crowd below, just in time, too. Surprise renders me immobile as I watch Solange cross the dance floor. When I broke it off with her yesterday, she swore to never forgive me, and yet she's here tonight. Sighing, I think about leaving to avoid the drama heading my way.

But instead of heading up the stairs, she stops to talk to Alric, a high-ranking vampire in our society, her gestures as dramatic and flamboyant as her nature. She's up to something. When she points across the room, I crane my neck to look, but I can't see it from where I'm standing. I hurry to the other side, but whatever or whoever is gone. I turn back to Solange to find her walking off, while Alric watches her go with longing in his eyes. The fool is in love with her. If she was smart, she'd realize that he's a suitable match for her.

I stroll back to where the cadre waits.

Theron is frowning at me. "What's wrong?"

"Solange is up to something," I admit. "We broke up yesterday, and she's here tonight. Like most vampires, she can be petty and vindictive when denied. She might be after Arden."

"Why would she want to hurt Arden?" Theron is vibrating with anger as he bites out his question.

Running my hands through my hair, I tell him, "Ever since their fight, she's been obsessed with Arden. I thought I'd defused the situation, but now I'm wondering what she's doing."

Astor storms over. "Why didn't you tell us? We would have banned her from The Abbey."

"I thought I took care of it," I tell him tightly. "Now, I'm not so sure. My gut is churning."

"You better hope she doesn't hurt Arden," Valerian bites out. The lights flicker, and he glowers at me.

Rolling my eyes, I turn to watch the dance floor while my mind turns over Valerian's words. What's up with Valerian and Arden? Does he like her? I know they spend a lot of time training together, but if he thinks he's the only one who wants Arden, he needs to look around. Theron is so transparent these days, he's become a mockery of his old self. And Astor, charming flirt extraordinaire, is dropping the façade to show his true self, especially when he's around Arden.

I'm so caught up in my thoughts, I miss the opening statement from the DJ. Astor's shadow flicks my ear.

"Pay attention!" he hisses, jerking his head to the dance floor, where Alric stands with Arden in his arms.

Every muscle in my body locks down. Arden stares up at Alric with a dreamy smile, her arms locked around his neck, and I roar with anger. What the hell is going on? Based on what I saw the other night, Arden can't be compelled, but her face indicates otherwise.

"What did the DJ say?" I bite out.

Astor's face is pale when he responds. "He said the performance is called The Mate's Kiss."

My stomach drops. Vampires have few rules, but those that exist are ironclad. If a potential partner accepts your request for the Mate's Kiss, no other vampire, including myself, may interfere. It's essentially a blood exchange from a vampire to his true love and a vow that ties their lifelines together. The other golden rule? You can't compel a partner to accept your proposal.

"You'd better restrain Valerian," I command Astor, my voice cold.

Valerian roars when he sees what's happening below, and the crowd quiets. Thankfully, Astor's spell holds him, for now.

I glare down at Alric. "As First Vampire, you must answer me truthfully. Did Arden say yes to The Mate's Kiss?"

He swallows, nervously searching the crowd. "Yes!" he shouts.

"Answer truthfully, and I'll let you live. Did you compel her?" I ask, my voice hard. "Did you allow anyone else to compel her?"

"No." His voice rings out truthfully.

Gripping the railing, I hang on to my control by a thread, my heart stuttering at the thought of Arden belonging to any vampire but me. A burning rage makes me want to kill every vampire in her radius, but none of this reflects in my voice as I say, "Proceed."

Theron stands coldly beside me. "If he bites her, I'll kill him."

"If we move on him, he could bite her before we get to him. If he bites her and he dies, Arden dies, too," I say bleakly. My mind racing, I sift through vampire rules, trying to find a loophole.

The music starts, and they dance. He won't bite her until the end of the song. It's the grand finale.

The crowd is quiet and their faces solemn as they silently protest this farce. I'm searching the crowd, looking for answers, when I run across Reyna and Cassandra standing together. It's enough of an anomaly to make me stop. My eyes watch, picking up the incremental movement of their lips and hands.

"Astor. What are they doing?" I subtly draw his attention to the two witches.

Astor's eyes narrow, and shadows slither around his feet in agitation. "Fuck me, they're using a spell. She's not compelled, she's bespelled. I'll kill them."

"Can you counter?" I ask desperately as the music is ending.

Astor pulls a knife out and draws a line across his palm, spilling blood. "I'll try."

With Astor focused on the witches, Valerian breaks his bonds and roars with fury. Standing at the railing, he shouts down to Alric, "If you bite her, I'll chain you to a forgotten cave in my kingdom, always hungry, always alone. There are worse things than death, Alric. Think about it."

Alric's steps falter as he looks for a savior, but the crowd doesn't offer any. The last bars of the song float in the air, and resigned, he pulls Arden's head back to expose her throat, then strikes…air. She's gone.

Arden appears by Valerian's side. He wraps his arms around her and shudders. "Fuck, lass. That was too damn close."

Relief weakens my knees, and I tighten my grip on the railing.

I reach out with my power to keep Solange and Alric from fleeing.

Arden is furious, and her power, no longer dampened, flows pure and strong. She steps over to Astor, and gives him a light kiss, bringing him out of his trance. "Thank you. I felt a prick on my hand, and everything turned hazy. The next thing I remember, I was on the dance floor in Alric's arms, trapped by spells. Cassandra and Reyna were working together to layer the spells one on top of the other. Every time I unraveled a spell from Cassandra, Reyna's spell would trap me again, over and over. Your magic disrupted theirs long enough for me to wrestle control back."

Astor gives her a deep kiss. "Stop giving me grey hair, gorgeous. It's not a good look for me."

Theron pulls her in close, his cool lips skimming down her

throat, replacing Alric's scent with his own. "I'm going to kill them." He's almost feral as his own Fae fangs drop, his famous control shattered.

Fallon pulls her in for a bone-crushing hug, his fury evident in the clenched hands and warrior stance he's held the entire time. He solemnly hands her to me.

"I'll make this right," I promise her. "Solange and Alric will pay."

She nods and steps back into Valerian's arms. "But the witches are mine."

Theron argues with her, but she shakes her head furiously. The witches left as soon as Astor broke their spell, so we missed capturing them.

Facing the crowd, I decide to address them all. "As you can see, this witch, Arden, is under our protection. We told you time and time again, and you ignored us. Did you forget who we are?" I roar with fury.

As First Vampire, I control all vampires. Most of the time, I leave them alone, but for those who break the rules, the consequences are severe. "Solange and Alric, step forward."

The crowd pushes Solange out onto the dance floor. Alric tries to grab her hand, but she shoves him away. Defiant, she spits out, "I'm not responsible for a witch using a spell on another witch."

Using sire compulsion to get her to tell the truth, I ask, "Did you compel Arden?"

"I tried, but she resisted," she admits.

"How did you get her to say yes to Alric's Mate Kiss request?" I demand.

She pinches her lips together to avoid answering, but it's useless, the truth spills out anyway. "The witches offered to use a spell to make her agreeable. See, I did nothing. It was the witches and Alric."

Alric pales. "I only did what you asked me to do, Solange."

"We'll deal with the witches. Compelling her to accept the Mate's Kiss violates our most sacred rules, even if you weren't successful," I pronounce. "The Mate's Kiss is sacred and not offered lightly, as it binds two lives together forever. It shouldn't be used for a petty act of revenge!" I shout, livid with her machinations. Solange and Alric flinch at my fury. "Instead of killing you like I want to, I'm going to give you a choice."

Both Solange and Alric look relieved, but Astor snorts. He knows me well enough to realize the choices will be abominable.

"You have two choices. Solange and Alric, you can say yes to each other's Mate Kiss and stay a part of the vampire society, or I'll banish you forever." My voice is calm while I explain their options. "You have a minute to decide."

Theron compresses his lips, furious with my leniency. If it was him, he'd kill them, but he doesn't understand the need vampires have for their hive. My hive is the cadre. They satisfy my need for a family. Vampires rarely live long without a hive. It's a slow death.

Alric smiles with relief, but Solange stands there shaking her head. "No, I'm supposed to be yours, not his. Our fathers are best friends. We grew up with each other. We are meant to be together. Please, please, Daire. We can get past this little incident. I love you," she pleads, tears rolling down her cheeks.

"We will never be together again," I tell her, my voice hard and emotionless. "You should accept Alric as your mate. He will provide you with a good life."

Solange stares at me in disbelief and anguish. "I will never belong to anyone but you. I refuse Alric." She takes a deep breath. "I choose banishment."

Alric's smile turns to horror as he realizes what she's decided. He grabs her shoulders. "Don't do this. We can be happy and alive." He pleads with her over and over.

She shakes him off and snarls at me, "Do it."

Sadly, I wonder what I could have done to prevent this from

happening. "Solange and Alric, I banish you both from vampire society and the hive. Nobody will speak to or acknowledge you after tonight. Nobody will offer you shelter or help of any kind. It will be as if you never existed."

Alric sways, then shuffles off the dance floor.

Solange glares up at me, then Arden. "You'll regret this moment. Like it or not, you'll be mine again." She strides off the dance floor, head held high.

Looking at the cadre, I silently ask for their agreement. All four heads nod. I glance at Arden, whose face is hard as she stares at the crowd. I turn and face the crowd, fangs flashing. "For your role in this fiasco, The Abbey is closed for a month. Let this be a warning. The next time someone messes with the cadre or anyone under our protection, we'll kill everyone involved and close The Abbey, permanently." The crowd is stunned. "The staff can stay. Everyone else needs to leave, now."

The crowd scatters, trying to be the first out the door and away from our wrath.

Calling Maya over, I tell her to give the staff full pay and a month's vacation.

She gives me a hard nod. "I'm sorry. I didn't realize what was happening until the music started. From now on, I'll vet all performances."

Theron steps up and stares at Maya impassively before giving her further instructions. "When you speak with the staff, tell them the petty acts against Arden stop now. I've been tolerant, more tolerant than I should have been, but I'm done. We're done. If they can't accept working with Arden, they can consider this pay their severance." He pauses, giving Maya the chance to agree. "And, Maya, letting these things happen is also grounds for dismissal. I expect more from you in the future."

Maya's shoulders slump for a second, then she straightens, nods determinedly, and strides off to speak to the staff.

I turn to Theron, but he's watching Maya's conversation with the staff. If there's a hint of disagreement, he'll notice it. After a second, the tension eases from his shoulders. Thankfully, nobody is stupid enough to test us today.

I squeeze Theron's shoulder, grab a bottle of Macallan, and offer Arden a drink.

She takes a long swig from the bottle, then hands it to Theron, who looks around for glasses.

Rolling her eyes, she laughs and turns to Valerian. "You still want me to take a week? Look what could have happened tonight. If we wait until the timing is perfect, we could wait forever or miss our chance. I don't need time to think about it. I know what I want."

He pulls her into his arms and lifts her chin. "You're right. We don't get any guarantees in life." He pauses, his face losing its grin. "And I promise to do everything in my power to give us time."

"I promise, too," Arden vows solemnly.

Valerian picks up Arden and heads toward the elevators.

I glance at Theron and Fallon. Oddly enough, there's a gleam of satisfaction in Theron's eyes, while Fallon's face is impassive.

But when I turn to joke with Astor, he's staring wistfully at them. I lock eyes with him and nod in understanding. Hybrids like Astor and myself don't know if we'll be lucky enough to mate. As a vampire, I'm given the option of giving my love a Mate's Kiss to bind our lifelines, but it doesn't bind our souls. Most demon and human hybrids, like Astor, don't even have that option.

I stare down into my drink, reliving tonight's roller coaster of emotions. The human part of us loves fiercely, but is that enough?

28

ARDEN

After setting me down inside his room, Valerian slowly lowers his mouth to mine, but a sudden thought has me stopping him. Puzzled, he leans back.

Valerian reads the hesitancy on my face and stiffens. "Lass? Do you need some more time to think about it?"

Thoughts race through my mind. I wonder if my mother and father were mates, or simply in love? Is one better than the other? A mate is bound to your soul, but if someone is bound to your heart, is it any less important? If a mate is willing to give you a piece of their soul and a lover a piece of their heart, I don't believe one piece is more valuable than the other. I have to tell him.

I lace my fingers together tightly. "I'm not sure. I need to talk to you about something, but I don't know how to start this conversation. Solandis and Vargas only wanted each other. They didn't want anyone else. They're not only mates, but they're deeply in love with each other." I pause to get some clarity and rein in my babbling. "I know our world, the supernatural world, allows for multiple mates. But what if someone isn't a mate? What if you love someone but they're not your mate, and you end up wanting to spend the rest of your life with them, too?"

He cocks his head to the side. "If you have another mate, I wouldn't stand in the way. If the fates have blessed you with more than one mate, we would work together to figure it out. It's the way it's always been." Licking his lips, he asks, "Do you think you have more than one mate? Are you having feelings for someone else?"

"Yes and yes," I answer truthfully. "I suspect I have another mate. But what if I'm also attracted to someone who isn't my mate? And what if, in the future, I fall in love with that person?"

He runs a hand over his face. "Who?"

I hesitate. "I don't want to say anything about the person who I suspect is my mate, not yet. It wouldn't be fair to him. But..." I need to stop making a mess and just blurt it out. "I'm attracted to Astor—deeply, insanely attracted. Something inside him calls to me. It's not just lust, although there's plenty of that, too. I don't know where it's going to go, maybe nowhere, but it feels like it has roots. I haven't told him. I can barely admit it to myself and to you." I stare into his amber eyes. "I want to be your mate. The fates wouldn't give us to each other if we weren't meant to be, but I can't let Astor go. So if you want to wait, I understand."

He stares down at me, his face expressionless. "Are you sure, lass? Astor has never known love at all, not from anyone, much less felt love for someone else. It might never happen. I don't want you to get your heart broken," he replies. Then he pauses to really think about it, and I can see he answer in his eyes, even before he tells me.

"Astor means a lot to me. He's my brother, my cadre, and I would love nothing more than to see him happy with anyone, which includes you, even if you're my mate. But I want you to be prepared."

"I am. I just have this feeling I can't explain. It's not love, not yet, and maybe not ever. I only know I have to try," I reassure him, relief filling my voice.

"Oh, lass. Let's hope Astor isn't the master of his own destruction," he says quietly. "Regardless, I'm glad you told me, and I'll be a lucky dragon if you're my mate. Can I kiss you now and find out?"

Without replying, I reach up and pull his lips down to meet mine in a passionate kiss. It's like meeting the sun. Desire pools between us, while an overwhelming feeling of warmth takes over my entire body. I can feel tiny threads from his soul reaching out and binding with mine. With our souls tethered, his essence pours through me, showing me everything about him. Valerian's soul is pure and light and filled with the ages of living. Mine is young in comparison, but they merge easily, as if they are the same. Amazed, I pull back and gaze up at him.

I see my feelings of wonder and awe reflected on his face. Still holding me in his arms, he stares down at me. "Lass, I can't believe I asked you to wait. When I saw you in Alric's arms, I wanted to rip his head off. I knew I wouldn't be able to make it in time. In that moment, I knew with every fiber of my being, I wanted you as my mate." He tucks a strand of hair behind my ear. "I promise you, I'm not a stupid man. Forgive me?"

Feeling sassy, I say, "Maybe. I see groveling in your future." Then I sober, thinking of the night's events. "We were pawns in other's agendas. Although Caro wasn't here, the witches wouldn't have moved against me if Caro hadn't approved it. I must have made her nervous. Guess I'll find out tomorrow."

He growls. "I don't like the thought of you going after them. Who are you planning to take with you?"

"I'm not going after them yet. I simply want them to know their plan failed. And I'm going to ask Astor to go with me.

They hate him, and I want my message to be loud and clear," I explain, my voice hard with fury.

Valerian picks me back up, kicks the door closed and sits down in the chair by the fireplace with me in his lap. "Lass, I want you here with me tonight. Even if it's just holding you tight, I need to feel you in my arms and next to me. Will you stay?"

"Are you going to carry me around forever?" I jokingly ask, but secretly, I love it. For a tall woman, I rarely get carried, and it makes me feel cherished and desired.

His arms tighten. "Until I can get Alric's face out of my mind, maybe."

I smooth the frown line between his brows before using my finger to trace his features. Mine. He's mine, and in a way nobody else has ever been. Although I love my adopted parents, I've never had someone to claim solely as my own, a person who's willing to stand beside me for the rest of my life. Whether it's short or long, he'll be there, and while neither of us love each other yet, the mate bond tethers us tightly together.

"Tell me," he demands, stroking my hair back from my face.

"You're the first person I've ever called mine. And as mates, we're bound by our souls for eternity, but I don't think mates are the only important connections. Giving someone a piece of your heart is equally important. Both bind you to a person. You loved Moira fiercely, and her you, and your love was strong and real. I'm amazed at this feeling of being your mate and I'll treasure it forever, but someday, I want your heart, too," I state quietly. "Not today, but one day, when nothing matters more than telling me you love me."

Valerian's amber eyes search mine before he nods. He pulls me close and captures my lips in a deep, luscious kiss. His pouty lips claim mine, sealing our pact with fire, imprinting his taste on my tongue.

He stands up and carries me over to the bed. Without

breaking our kiss, he lowers us down, settling between my legs. For eons, we kiss, learning and savoring each other, grateful for this pause before the storm. We break and stare at each other, the silence only broken by the sound of our breathing.

His amber eyes are darker, closer to molten gold. I inhale, and my breath catches. Mine, he's all mine. I don't realize I'm saying the words until he repeats them. A tidal wave of desire sweeps us up, immediate and all-consuming. We dive into each other, clothes flying everywhere, hands touching with uncontrollable frenzy.

"Lass, I want to learn every inch of your body, map it like it's my own. But right now, I just need...to be inside of you," he rasps. He slips down to my core and licks my slit from top to bottom.

Gasping, my legs fall open, making room for him. "Hurry," I plead. With a tug on his hair, I bring him to my clit, moaning when he circles it with his tongue. "More."

He picks up my hips, bringing my pussy up to his lips to devour every inch of me, licking, sucking, and nibbling on my clit, then fucking me with his tongue. It's been so long and I'm so turned on, it takes a mere minute for me to come.

My hands clench the sheets as I buck up into his mouth. My orgasm rolls through my body, and I moan.

He continues to kiss and taste me until he feels the tremors subside. "You're so beautiful when you come," he drawls huskily. Sliding up my body, he positions his cock at my entrance and slowly slides into me.

Moaning, I shift and widen my legs to pull him closer. He's so big, his cock stretching me, making me restless for him to move. "Fuck, you're big, dragon. I need you to move, but slowly."

He grins and slides out an inch. He groans. "Damn, lass, you're so tight. Give me a second." With a slow inhale, he pulls out halfway, then slides back in. "Fuck me, you feel so good. Maybe too damn good."

He continues to give me time to adjust with slow thrusts. Sweat beads on his brow as he rocks back and forth, his cock getting harder with each pass.

My body finally loosens its stranglehold, and all I feel is pleasure. "Harder. When you slide back in, I need it harder."

In the middle of pulling out, he thrusts in hard and groans. His pure gold eyes stare down at me, cataloguing every response. "I love sliding in and out of your pussy. It's so slick. My cock wants to slide out to the tip, feeling every quiver on my shaft, before slamming back into you, diving deep until my balls meet your ass." He groans. "And then do it all over again."

"Valerian," I breathe, and my pussy flutters around his cock. "More."

"I need to be deeper," he rasps and withdraws. He quickly picks me up, flips me to my knees and sinks back into me. "Not enough." Grabbing a pillow, he places it under my hips, angling me almost straight up, and slams into me. "That's it, lass. I'm so deep inside you, I can't feel where I end and you begin. And your ass...so beautiful." He caresses my ass as he slides in and out.

"Stop playing," I demand. "I'm so close, Valerian. My mate. Mine. Fuck me." Incoherent words spill out of my mouth. The edge is right in front of me, I just need him to move faster.

He moans. "Say it again. Mine. I need to hear you're mine." His hips piston back and forth as he picks up speed. His fingers find my clit, and he strokes it until I come.

"I'm yours. Your mate. Valerian!" I scream as I come hard, pushing back to take every inch of him into me. My pussy clenches his cock, triggering his own release.

He roars, thrusting a couple more times before he stops, buried deep inside me. His forehead rests on my back, and his breathing is harsh while he slowly calms. "You're mine. My mate," he murmurs over and over before pulling out.

I groan and fall to the bed facedown.

He rolls me over, sweeps my hair out of my eyes, and kisses me. "I'm going to enjoy being your mate, lass. That was incredible, but I think we can do better, don't you?"

"My dragon," I muse, running my finger lightly over his lips. With the edge off, I'm ready for round two. "Want to join me for a shower?"

He's out of bed in a flash. Swooping down, he picks me up and carries me into the bathroom, where a massive shower waits for us.

29

ARDEN

Deliciously sore after spending the night with Valerian, I'm heading back to my room for a shower when I see Astor in the hallway. I hurry to catch up to him.

His dark brown eyes gleam when they spot me. "Hello, gorgeous. You're looking delightfully fucked this morning," he purrs. Stepping in close, he takes a deep breath and moans. "I can smell the sex on you, the sweet scent of your pussy mixed with Valerian's cock. It makes the incubus in me desperate to lay you on the floor and lick up all the sexual magic that's dripping out of you." His tongue flicks over my lips, sipping from them.

As if his words aren't enough, he uses our shared power to make me visualize his head between my legs, his tongue licking up every drop. I moan. "Astor, stop. I don't have time for this right now. I need to ask you for a favor."

"A favor, huh? This morning is getting better and better," he quips. "What can we do for each other?"

"I'm going to visit Reyna and Cassandra," I reply. "I want you to go with me."

He pulls back and snarls, "No. You ask too much. I haven't stepped foot in Witchwood since I was seven. Ask Theron to go with you." He walks away.

I take two steps to catch up to him. "Wait. Please," I beg. "Is there nothing I can do to convince you to go with me? I need someone who pisses them off, and your very existence is an affront to their exclusive bullshit. I'm declaring war, not negotiating, and you're better suited for that goal than Theron."

He breathes in deeply but doesn't move. "You greatly underestimate Theron. That bastard is one of the finest warriors I've ever met," he remarks.

I slide my hand down his arm and lace my fingers through his. "Really? I'm not sure I see it. Besides, Theron's icy etiquette is too subtle for this visit. I need someone who doesn't give a shit about appearances."

He turns and backs me into the wall. "You ask a lot, more than you know. I swore to myself I'd never step foot into there again." His face twists with memories. "What's my incentive?"

"What do you want?" I cry.

"I want to taste you now, before you shower. I want to fuck you with my tongue," he snaps back. "Then, I want one night with you, completely under my control. A night of my choosing. No regrets. No declarations of love. Just you, me, and my incubus."

My mind fills with images of us together in positions I've never even tried, and I moan, turned on by his words and those scenes. "Yes," I breathe. Haven't I already been thinking this same thing?

"Shouldn't you check with your mate?" he whispers harshly in my ear.

"Valerian knows I want you. He's fine with it," I admit breathlessly.

The words are barely out of my mouth before he's throwing me over his shoulder. I hang down his back, bouncing, while he stalks down to my room. Smacking his ass, I demand, "Let me up, Astor. I didn't agree to be carried like a sack of potatoes."

He doesn't reply. Reaching my room, he enters and flings me down onto the bed. He drops to his knees, jerks me to the edge of the bed, then shoves my skirt to my waist. I hear my panties ripping a second before his tongue spears into my sensitive pussy.

"Astor," I whisper harshly.

"Fuck, your pussy tastes so good with Valerian's cum all over you. I can taste the sex and magic you two generated last night." His voice deepens, no longer the smooth cadence of Astor's. Instead, his incubus is now in control. He spreads my legs wide and licks every inch of me. "Mmm. I bet that massive cock of his stretched your pussy wide. Tell me."

"No, that's between Valerian and me," I say, denying his request.

He roars.

Magic wafts over me, making me pulse and clench. Need pounds in me, and I grit my teeth. "I didn't agree to share details from my night with Valerian. Are you voiding our deal?"

"No." His voice guttural when he replies. "Deal is deal." With that sullen agreement, he renews licking and sucking my pussy, taking me over the edge several times before I cry for mercy. Finally, he releases me.

Astor helps me sit up, and I fall boneless against him. With quick hands, he undresses me, then steps into the shower with me. He washes me tenderly, even shampooing my hair, before he helps me out. A snap of his fingers, and we're dry.

The snap jolts me out of my lethargic mood. With a glare at him, I practically stomp over to the closet.

"There you are, gorgeous," he drawls sexily. "I thought I'd broken you."

"A fuck ton of orgasms in one night and a morning will do that to a girl," I snarl.

I pull a pair of black leather leggings out of the closet, along with a skin-tight black T-shirt and my black combat boots. A scarf easily hides my rune. No need to let Caro know about my built-in alarm system. Armor in place, I grab Astor's hand and take him with me.

30

ARDEN

Astor's sexual high is so strong, it's almost suffocating. I wave a hand in the air, dispersing the surrounding cloud, and he grins broadly.

"This is only the tip of the cock, gorgeous," he jokes. "Sadly, while I will cherish the memory of your taste forever, the magic will only last a couple of days, but thoughts of our night together will sustain my imagination for weeks. And when it happens, it's going to feed my power for a fucking month."

Rolling my eyes at his outlandish statements, I pull him into the portal I've created. We're going to Santiago and Reyna's house, first.

When the Spanish villa comes into sight, I jog up to the gate and lay my finger on the button.

"Hello?" an older lady's voice asks.

"Hello," I reply sweetly. "Is Reyna home?"

"May I ask who's calling?" the voice responds.

"Oh, it's her dear friend, Arden." I pause. "And Astor."

A minute goes by without a sound from the intercom. Then I see Reyna opening the front door and walking towards the gate. I guess she's not inclined to let us in. That's okay.

I cross my arms and widen my stance. "You've got one chance to tell me what happened and why. If you don't, I'll tell the council your family is descended from shifters." It's purely a guess, but a good one, judging by the expression on her face. It occurred to me when Santiago was teaching me how to transfigure. They call it transfigure or transform, only because they can turn into any living creature, unlike a shifter, who can only shift into one animal, but it's no different.

"Please. You can't tell anyone," she cries. Throwing up her hands, she stalks to the gate and grips the metal rails in her fists. "Cassandra told me to help her put a spell on you that would make you accept Alric's proposal."

My anger skyrockets with her words. Even though I knew she did it, it still stings to hear it. "Why would you do anything Cassandra told you to do? I thought you hated her." I fling my words at her while my magic brushes against her shield, testing its strength. It's weak, weaker than it should be when standing at the gate with your enemy in front of you.

"I do," she says vehemently, her jaw tight. "She's blackmailing me. If I don't do what she says, she'll tell her mom about Jax and me. Then Caro will banish me from the coven."

"Jax?" I ask, confused as to who Jax might be, but not surprised to hear about Cassandra blackmailing Reyna.

"My ex-boyfriend, Jax. He's an incubus," she breathes with a glance towards Astor.

Seriously? "Who cares who you date?" I throw my hands in the air. "Is this more of the coven's exclusive bullshit?"

"You don't understand. When you're cut off from the coven, you're cut off from every person you care about in the world. The coven's not great, but it's all I've got," she cries. She swipes her arm over her face to dry her tears, and I stare at her. She's broken by the coven, and she doesn't even know it.

"I'm going to let you in on a little secret. You don't need a coven to be a powerful witch. You just need family. Whether it's the family you're born to or one you create for yourself, family provides the power for your magic. From what I've seen, the coven takes a lot from you. Are you sure they're giving you enough in return?"

Astor steps up and pulls me close. I glance up at him and realize this is hard for him to hear, too. I link my fingers with his and pull them up to my mouth for a kiss. Let Reyna see. I give zero fucks. His eyes shine with disbelief.

"Reyna, I feel sorry for you, I do, but if you ever try to cast a spell on me again, I'll kill you. Remember that promise when Cassandra's blackmailing you. Banishment might be better than death, but if it's not, I'll be happy to help you make that decision," I threaten, then I turn towards the road to create a portal, but her voice stops me.

"Wait. I told Caro about the Killian blades I saw in your room!" she shouts. "She wants them, badly."

Fuck me. No wait, fuck her. I swing around and fling a spell at her, piercing her shield with ease. Needle and thread appear and sew her lips together. "Don't worry, the spell will dissolve when you see your father and tell him everything—what you did to me, your love for your incubus, and the fact Cassandra's blackmailing you. If you don't spill everything, your mouth will remain sewn shut. I heard your dad is going to be back tomorrow?" She nods with a sniff. "Good. That's enough time for you to think long and hard about your current path. Good luck." I spin on my heel and open a portal to Witchwood, Astor's hand still clasped in mine.

"Bravo, gorgeous," Astor whispers in my ear. He tries to untangle his fingers from mine as we walk through the portal.

"What are you doing?" I ask, gesturing to our hands.

"As much as I appreciate your declaration, let's keep it on the down low for now…hmm?" he suggests. "We don't want to push Caro over the edge before your placement ceremony, do we?"

"No, you're right," I respond. "But when all this is over…"

Astor nods, and a small smile of satisfaction appears. "Shall we?" He gestures to the door of Witchwood.

Unlike Reyna's house, Witchwood's gates are wide open, the wards programmed to let witches pass. Startled, I glance at Astor and raise my eyebrows. I didn't think about it the first time I visited because I didn't feel any wards. This time, though, the wards are up, and yet, they let me and my mixed blood right in, and Astor, too. The magic recognizes witches, and pure or mixed blood doesn't seem to matter, which makes sense, if my theory is correct.

Henry opens the door. "Good afternoon, Miss Arden. Mr. Astor. Do you have an appointment?"

I decide to ignore his question. "Is Caro home?"

"Yes, Miss Arden. She's in the Heritage Room," he replies. "Please, follow me."

"Thanks, Henry," I say warmly. We follow Henry to the room, where he announces us to Caro.

Startled, she tries to block us from the room. "We don't allow outsiders to see this room. It contains our witch heritage."

"Really, am I included in that heritage?" Astor asks, stepping into the room.

Incensed, Caro stalks over to him. "I'm going to have to ask you to leave," she demands.

My eyes are drawn to the large tapestry hanging on the wall depicting a massive family tree. I walk up to view it closer. "What is this?" Entranced, I trace each family's branch. A leaf on the Perrone branch says Gia Perrone with the day and year of her birth and death on it.

Caro stands stiffly beside me. "It's the rowan tree, our coven's tree. It lists every witch ever born," she answers. With a glance at Astor, she amends her statement. "Every pure witch."

As I turn my head towards her, my peripheral vision catches a micro-thin layer on top of the tapestry. It shimmers like a second skin, almost entirely translucent. My eyes widen when I realize it's a concealment spell. Is it a spell Caro knows about or not?

A bowl with a thorn in the center sits on the table beneath the tapestry. Centuries of dried blood has turned it black. I think this is the bowl Cassandra mentioned to me. "What's this?" I reach out to touch the bowl, but Caro grabs my hand.

"We use that during the placement ceremony," she says. "It confirms you are a witch, with witch powers, and it accepts or rejects you into the coven."

The bowl just became infinitely more interesting to me. "Do you know your daughter drugged me, then placed a spell on me to make me accept a vampire's Mate Kiss?" I drop the question into the discussion without fanfare.

"What? You must be mistaken. Cassandra would never drug or place a spell on another witch, especially without my knowledge," she states. "I assume you have proof?"

I glance at Astor, who narrows his eyes, and remarks, "Unfortunately, they disappeared before we could catch them, along with any proof that might have lingered."

Caro sneers at Astor. "They?"

"Reyna Santiago was with her," he sneers back.

Caro scoffs. "As if you have any right to hold my daughter or Reyna in your custody. Witches fall under coven rules."

"The cadre is the ultimate power at The Abbey. Please tell Cassandra I'm looking for her. If she steps foot in our sanctuary again, I'll be waiting," he requests with a sinister smile. "The next time it happens, we'll kill everyone involved. Nobody messes with those under our protection."

"Who's under your protection?" she asks, laughing.

"I am," I answer softly. I glance at Astor. "We're done here." A couple of steps brings me to the door. "Oh and, Caro, the Killian blades found me, not the other way around. I wouldn't mess with them, if I were you. They have a nasty habit of killing everyone, not just the Fae."

31

ARDEN

My mind is ticking over the facts I know so far. I grab a piece of paper and a pen to write down my thoughts—the MacAllisters, Amelie's mixed Fae and witch heritage, the likelihood of the Santiagos having mixed shifter and witch heritage, the tapestry and thorn bowl, the power the light has over the dark, and the beliefs the witches have about power and purity.

I still feel like I'm missing part of the puzzle—my part. I sigh and realize the only option is to go through with the placement ceremony. It's the only way I'll know where I fit in this fucked up ball of yarn. I stand and stretch. There's only one item left on my to do list. I stroll out of the room to find Daire.

He responds immediately to my text with his location and directions. I haven't been to his room yet, so this should be interesting.

I open the door, then immediately close it. I must have taken a wrong turn somewhere. My eyes scan the hallway for another door, but one doesn't appear. With a frown, I reach for the doorknob just as Daire opens it from the other side.

"What are you doing?" he asks, staring down at me.

While Theron and Astor are only a couple of inches taller than me, I realize that Daire is about five or six inches taller. Not quite as tall as Valerian or Fallon, but enough to make me feel less like an Amazon.

He smiles hesitantly. "Arden? Do you want to go somewhere else?"

"What?" I say, snapping out of my daze. "No, this is good. Thank you." I wait for him to invite me into his room—his pitch-black room. If this was Astor's room, I'd understand, but it doesn't feel like Daire. Even though Daire is a vampire, he's full of light and snark, not shadows and darkness like Astor. Yet, this is his room. It even smells like him and the expensive cologne he wears. I wonder if he has any scent without the cologne? Most vampires don't, but Daire is also half witch.

He pulls me over to a luxurious black leather couch, where a knife sits next to a bowl. "I've prepared some tools, so we can create wounds and heal them. Please, have a seat. I'll text Theron."

I tense, remembering the last time I was near the two. My knees fold, and I sink down into the couch. It's cool to the touch. "Good thinking," I tentatively state. "Okay, let's get started. Unfortunately, the ceremony is tomorrow, so I only have today to get this right."

He tilts his head to assess me. "You're tense. The first time you heal, it's better if you're calm."

I take a deep breath before explaining, "I think it's this room. It doesn't feel like you, and it's kind of freaking me out."

Startled, he scans the room. "Why do you feel it's not me? I decorated it."

"You did?" I snort. "I thought Solange decorated this room. It feels like her."

"Well, we were dating," he says dryly. "She had a lot of input. What do you think my room should look like?"

With a shrug, I glance around at the cold, dark interior. "It should be warm. When you get angry, you don't coat the walls with ice, like Theron, or shadows, like Astor. You burn with the hottest of flames, a blue flame. And with all your golden looks, the black washes you out. I think you need a room filled with blues, in various shades. Something that speaks to your heart and who you are." I stop and blush. Did I go too far?

A slow smile takes over his face. "I'll consider it. If this place makes you uncomfortable, where do you want to go?"

I think about it. "I'm not sure. I haven't been to many places in The Abbey. Is there someplace to relax?"

He picks up the bowl and knife. "Follow me," he calls, striding out of the room. We enter the elevator, and with a murmur, we're traveling to our destination.

The doors open to lush greenery and an abundance of flowers. I gasp. "This is beautiful," I exclaim. "I didn't know we had a garden!" I slip off my shoes, step on the grass, and wiggle my toes. "This is heaven." I laugh and twirl while Daire stares at me like I'm crazy.

He rolls his eyes, making fun of my childlike appreciation for the garden, but I see the smile he fails to hide. His hand motions me over to a few chairs sitting in the grass. "It's mostly used by Theron and Fallon when they need nature to help them rejuvenate. And Astor uses it to grow some of his herbs for potions." He points to a greenhouse in the corner. "But I must confess, I often forget it's here."

We both sit, and he pulls up a table to set the knife and bowl on it before texting Theron with our new location.

My anxiety vanishes. "This is much better." I pause, thinking about how that sounded. "I'm sorry about bashing your room.

And since I'm apologizing, I'm also sorry about you and Solange breaking up. I can almost understand why she went a little crazy after losing you."

"That's very sweet, but I wasn't in love with her. I should have broken it off a long time ago, but I didn't want the drama, so I ignored the situation. Alric almost tied your life to his because of my mistake. It will be a while before I forgive myself," he says, his voice vibrating with anger.

"You and Solange didn't seem like you really fit. Maybe I just don't know her that well?" I tentatively state.

His eyes are distant when he answers my unspoken question. "Solange's father and mine are best friends, and him and his wife have spent a lot of time at our house. One day, her father adopted this tiny abandoned vampire, named Solange. She was a charming child, full of recklessness and laughter, and we were all enamored of her. And even though I was quite a bit older, she took to following me everywhere. Once she grew up, we were often thrown together at Underworld high society events. My memories of her as a child and the beautiful woman she grew into somehow blended together. I saw what I wanted to see. Unfortunately, along the way she changed, became spoiled and power hungry. I really am sorry."

"Please, stop. I'm feeling very lucky these days. The cadre has given me a lot—sanctuary, a home, friends, and a mate. Theron and Fallon work night and day to follow up on the assassination leads. Valerian and Astor spend time to train me every day. You've healed me, and now you're going to teach me to heal. That's more than I expected when I came here to ask for help," I say softly. "I forgive you. I don't forgive the witches or Solange and Alric. But we can discuss that another day. Let's get started."

He studies my face for a minute without saying a word. Finally, he says, "Okay, to heal, you need to let your heart lead. If it's a stranger, think about them having a family or being their doctor, something that makes you have warm feelings towards them. For those you know, bring up happy or loving memories of them, or think good thoughts about them. Then think about how much you want them to get better." With a swift movement, he reaches out and cuts my hand.

Shocked, I glare at him.

"Remember this feeling," he demands. His hand reaches over and covers mine. A glow engulfs my hand, and I feel an overall warmth coming from him, then the wound knits together.

I turn my hand over and examine it for any sign of the injury, but I find none. Even though I'm immortal, it's amazing to me.

"Now, I texted Theron and asked him to volunteer. I can't be healed by magic anymore. My father's blood took over a long time ago," he states matter-of-factly, as if it doesn't bother him anymore.

Theron steps off the elevator and strides over to us. He eyes the knife on the table with distaste before pulling up another chair. With a wave of his hand, his feet are shoeless and buried in the grass like mine.

I smirk at his small display of abandonment. He raises an eyebrow, and I glance down at my feet. His eyes follow, then gleam with happiness to find me barefoot in the grass, too.

"Thank you for volunteering," I say with a chuckle. Looking at Daire, I motion for him to continue.

"Slice his hand and think about what I told you—memories, feelings, anything that makes you feel warmly towards Theron," he dictates.

Without giving myself too much time to think about it, I slice Theron's palm. He doesn't even flinch, just gazes at me steadily.

His blood flows onto the grass. Startled at the sight of the dark red against the bright green, I think about the fact that he's not wearing any shoes in the grass. I like this less restrained version of him, and I smile.

I feel warmth crawling from my heart to my hand. A second

later, a glow appears and then stops. When I take my hand away, the cut is healed. I stare at it in wonder, running my fingers softly over his unmarked skin. As a witch, I'm used to using magic to battle and cause damage or for mundane tasks. But healing, it's powerful. I look up at Daire in awe.

"This is incredible," I whisper, not willing to disturb the peace of the moment.

"It's truly a gift," he murmurs. "One I thought I'd lost a long time ago. You gave it back to me. It's only right I give it to you."

We stare at each other, a new awareness growing between us.

Theron clears his throat. "Do you need anything else?"

Daire smiles at him, and all I see is a blur.

Theron yells, "What the hell, Daire?" He grabs the handle of the knife stuck deep in his stomach and yanks it out. Cursing, he slaps a hand on the gushing wound and slams the knife on the table.

Daire quietly reminds me. "Stay calm, Arden. This is going to take a lot more power than the paltry cut you gave him a second ago, but we don't know what the witches might ask you to heal. You can do this. Think about Theron."

Peering up at the ceiling for answers, I try to calm down. Seeing Theron seriously wounded is pushing a button I didn't know was there. Shaky, I concentrate on breathing. In, out.

Theron stumbles to his feet. "It's okay. I can just go lie down. I'll heal."

I stand and grab his hips. "Please, sit back down. Let me try." I hold on to him as he eases back into the chair. My eyes meet Theron's violet eyes, and I think about all the times he protected me, stood up for me, helped me find my way. Lastly, I remember the wild look in his eyes when he gazed down at me in Alric's arms. My hands glow, and the wound closes.

He gasps. Standing, he rips his shirt off, pulling at his stomach to find the wound, but it's completely gone. "Thank you, Arden. I'm glad I could help you, but if you'll excuse me, I have somewhere I need to be." He strides off, half-naked.

"Do you think he's okay?" I ask, startled.

Daire lifts his shoulders. "Theron cloaks his feelings in duty and honor. One day, he won't be able to keep them contained in their self-designed box. Heaven help the person," Daire cuts his eyes to mine, "or woman responsible for lighting that fuse."

Hmmm.

Changing the topic, I jump up and launch myself into Daire's arms. "Thank you, thank you. I'm going to nail those final bloodline tests tomorrow. Is there anything I can do for you?"

He shakes his head. "You already did," he murmurs.

32

THERON

"When Daire and I worked together to help Arden learn to heal yesterday, I realized something." I pause and stare at each of my brothers, trying to convey the seriousness of what I'm about to say. "We're stagnant. Our bond is lax. We created the cadre and this bond between us to be a force to help others, to be an ally to those individuals standing alone. And for a long time, we did. Then, we settled down at The Abbey, and for the first five hundred years, we continued our work, using this sanctuary as a beacon to draw those in need."

I tap my fingers on the conference table in front of me. "Until now. We've become complacent. The pressures of running The Abbey, the toll of being a king or prince and the unending thirst for knowledge became the cornerstones of our days. We no longer searched the crowd for supernaturals who needed us. We turned inward." I frown, showing them my disappointment in the cadre and in myself. "Until Arden. Arden has given us back our purpose. She's strengthening our bond, reminding us why we created this cadre in the first place—to help other supernaturals like we once helped each other."

Fallon blinks. "You're right. Even though I'm here, at The Abbey, my mind and energy are with my father. I have resources out looking for Arden's assassins, but I've taken a passive approach, letting them come to me with updates instead of chasing them down. I continue to let my father's missions rule my life." Shame fills his face. "And I haven't taken the time to really get to know Arden. I promised to show her my powers, to see if they resonate, and I've done nothing."

I clap him on the back. "You're not the only one. Instead of delegating my daily duties, I embraced them, hiding behind the familiar while giving her help from the sidelines. And it's my life debt!" I pound my fist on the table, anger overriding my usual impassiveness. I watch them glance at each other, shocked by my emotion. "It stops now. Arden's important, not just because she needs us, but because we need her. She's Valerian's mate. His mate! And she's slowly claiming Astor, too. She's making us stronger, all of us." I glance at Astor, who's startled by my statement.

"She gave me the ability to heal again, my light, the one I've missed for so long," Daire admits softly.

Valerian's voice is gruff as he chimes in to the conversation. "Even before I knew she was my mate, I could see she was changing us in little and big ways. For me, I'd grown weary of the dragons and their resentment, but instead of looking for solutions, I let the status quo remain. Now? Arden's life could be in more danger simply for being my mate, and I have no relationships, no bargaining power with the dragons." He sighs heavily.

"When we visited the witches the other day, Arden held my hand in front of them proudly," Astor muses darkly. "And she encouraged Reyna, her enemy, to fight for her incubus lover without an ounce of prejudice."

Knowing we need more time, I propose a solution. "The Abbey is closed for a month. With your agreement, I propose we keep it closed for a while longer, which will give us time to focus on Arden." After getting their agreement, I lay out the next step. "Tomorrow is an important night for Arden. Hopefully, it's the beginning of some answers. I intend to stand by her side."

Valerian stands. "I'll be there. Arden has already told me she wants to introduce me as her mate. She says it will help to have the King of Dragons by her side." He snorts. "Vargas taught her battle strategy well, but strategy is not the reason I'm attending. As if I'd let my mate walk into that den of snakes alone."

Fallon straightens his shoulders. "I'll go. And starting next week, I'll show her my Elven magic. Maybe something in her will respond. I'll also put a hold on my father's missions for a while."

"I want to see her pass her healing test, and I want to stand up for her. Nobody stood for my mother when she tried to come back and present me to the coven...a mixed breed child," Daire rasps, the memories still painful. He looks over at Astor, who shares his pain.

With a grimace, Astor waves a hand. "I'll go." He leaves the simple statement hanging in the air.

"It's settled. I've got a few phone calls to make before tomorrow. We'll meet on the first floor by the elevators about thirty minutes before our departure time," I state. "After tomorrow night, we'll regroup and figure out our next steps with Arden."

33

ARDEN

With a turn, I survey myself in the mirror. My hands tremble as I smooth the amber silk dress over my hips. *Inhale, one, two, three, four, five. Exhale.* Besides the tremble in my hands, none of my internal turmoil is on display. My power is contained...for now.

Walking out of my room, I step inside the elevator to take it to the first floor of The Abbey. The doors open, and surprise renders me motionless for a brief second before I'm hurtling myself at the vision in front of me.

"Solandis!" I cry, diving into her arms. "What are you doing here? Not that I don't want you here, I do, but is it safe?"

After a long hug, she pulls back and holds me at arm's length. "Oh, sweetheart. Hardly any time has passed, and yet I feel like I'm seeing an entirely different person. You look beautiful, but there's something else, I can't quite put my finger on it."

Her eyes sweep over me from head to toe, and a tiny frown appears between her eyes.

"Give her to me," a gruff voice demands.

With tears in my eyes, I turn and step into Vargas' arms and the massive hug I know is waiting for me. "Vargas!" For a minute, I just allow him to hold me. I missed him and our daily sparring. I laugh. "I have someone for you to meet. Actually, more than one." A lone tear runs down my face, and I quickly swipe it away.

All five of the Imperium Cadre are standing a few feet away, their gazes glued to our family reunion. When I gesture to them, they step forward.

"Solandis, Vargas," I begin, my mind racing to figure out the best way to introduce them. "Meet the Imperium Cadre, my—" I stop and gather my thoughts. "Friends doesn't seem big enough to encompass everything they are to me. I'll just introduce them one by one."

Grabbing Valerian's hand, I pull him forward. Vargas' eyes widen, and he stands tall, puffing out his chest and widening his stance. "This is Valerian, King of Dragons and my mate." I let that sink in for a second.

Solandis gracefully steps up and takes Valerian's hand. "Welcome to the family," she says, warmth and happiness filling her voice. She steps back and elbows Vargas.

Vargas steps forward and shakes Valerian's hand. Based on Valerian's grunt, I assume it was one of Vargas' bone-crushing, 'we'll talk later' handshakes. He steps back and gives Valerian a hard stare.

I laugh. The fact that Vargas is restraining himself means he approves of our match and that Valerian is one of the few males Vargas actually respects.

A step to Valerian's right is Theron. Wrapping my hand in the crook of his elbow, I bring him forward. "You know Theron," I state. "He's been incredible, organizing us all and supporting me.

He's special to me." The simple statement is only the tip of the iceberg, barely conveying what he means to me, but I don't want to make Theron uncomfortable.

Theron's inscrutable violet eyes cut over to me, then to Solandis and Vargas. He bows deeply in front of Solandis. "I'm so glad you could make it. I know Arden has missed you very much."

Solandis smiles and takes his hand in hers. "Thank you for inviting us and for honoring your debt. You're more than I hoped for when I sent her to you."

Theron gives her another bow before turning to Vargas. He holds out his hand.

I stop breathing and look at Vargas. None of the Fae have ever offered to shake his hand. Most Fae hate him because he took their princess away.

Vargas tilts his head, assessing the sincerity of the offer, then slowly reaches out to grasp Theron's hand.

Feeling the awkwardness in the air, I grab Daire's hand and pull him over. Vargas has known him for a long time. "Daire, of course." I keep Daire's left hand clasped in mine, sending Vargas a statement without saying a word.

Vargas shakes Daire's hand. "Good to see you, Prince Daire." His eyes cut to mine as he emphasizes Daire's title.

I just smile and pull him over to Solandis. She gives him a warm smile, while her eyes stray to our joined hands. "Good to see you, Prince Daire," she says, deliberately using his title.

Leaving Daire with them, I reach out and motion for Astor to step forward. He sighs, giving the impression that he's impatient with these introductions. I lace my fingers with his and pull him forward.

"Solandis, Vargas, this is Astor, my lover," I say cheerfully. "Or soon to be lover, I guess, and my friend and magic trainer."

Astor stiffens and eyes Solandis and Vargas warily.

Solandis glances over at Valerian to gauge his reaction to my statement, but Valerian smiles back at her. She dips her chin to Astor and welcomes him into our family, before raising an eyebrow towards me.

Hmmm, I need to have a long talk with Solandis and Vargas, I muse.

Vargas smiles knowingly at Astor. "Arden's drawn to the darkness and shadows. I can see why she is drawn to you." He holds his hand out for Astor to shake.

Astor stares at him in shock, shakes his hand, then turns to me. I laugh and shrug. It's true. My fascination started with Vargas himself. He could be a loving parent to me, then go out and brutally execute someone.

Fallon steps up, a single eyebrow raised with a question in the depths of his eyes.

"This is Prince Fallon." I start my introduction with his proper title since we're still getting to know each other. A glint of sadness enters his eyes, then vanishes, and I frown. I didn't mean to imply he wasn't important to me. "He's my warrior friend, who's working hard to find my assassins. Vargas, please share any information you have with him."

Bemused, Fallon winks at me. He straightens his shoulders and holds his hand out for Vargas to shake. "Nice to meet you. Any information you can provide will help me hunt her assassins down."

Vargas assesses him, then shakes his hand. "It will be nice to have help. Neither Callyx nor myself have made much progress in finding the source, but I can show you every lead we've uncovered and discarded."

Solandis gives Fallon a radiant smile. "Thank you for helping Arden. She means everything to us."

Glancing at my phone, I realize we're running a few minutes behind. "Okay, we need to decide who's going to Witchwood with me." I look around at all the faces, almost everyone I care about most, with only Callyx missing. He'd called earlier and mentioned he would be busy with an important mission from Lucifer.

Theron places my hand in the crook of his arm. "We're all going."

I swallow the lump in my throat and smile. "Caro said I could bring my family."

34

ARDEN

Witchwood draws my eyes like a magnet when I step out of the portal. The mansion is lit up with cars parked along the driveway. Looks like a lot of witches are here tonight. Is this the normal attendance whenever a new witch joins the coven, or did Caro send out the word for backup?

The scent of burnt cedar fills the air. I turn and assess Astor. "Are you going to be okay tonight? You and Daire don't have to come."

Daire turns when I mention his name. His jaw is tight, but he looks determined. "We're going."

Astor nods. "What he said."

"In that case, I have a job for you," I whisper to Astor. Leaning closer, I tell him what I need him to do. When I pull away, I raise my eyebrow, asking if he can do it.

"My pleasure, gorgeous," he murmurs, pulling my hand up to place a kiss on it.

I smile and gesture towards the driveway. "Shall we?"

Henry is standing on the steps waiting for us to arrive. When he sees my entourage, he chuckles. "Good evening, Miss Arden. Everyone's waiting for you in the Heritage Room. Please, let me announce you...and your family." He sounds almost giddy with delight at the thought of announcing everyone.

We follow him to the Heritage Room, where he stops inside of the doorway. "Miss Arden, and her family." His voice rings out in the vast room, announcing us as we enter.

Conversation halts, and all eyes turn towards us. Caro, along with her husband and Nico Perrone, stride angrily over to us. "What is the meaning of this? We don't allow outsiders into our sacred ceremonies." Her eyes dart nervously to Solandis and Vargas.

"It was my understanding that I could bring my family. Is that not correct?" I project my voice, letting everyone hear my words.

"Of course you can bring family," Santiago states loudly. "Would you introduce us?" He steps out of the crowd, Reyna by his side. Her mouth is bare of the threads that were there the last time I saw her.

"These are my guardians." I gesture to Solandis and Vargas. "The Princess of the Light Fae and her mate, Vargas Karth, raised me from infancy." I pull Valerian forward. "This is my mate, Valerian, King of Dragons."

The crowd moves restlessly at my announcement. Caro frowns.

"And except for Callyx, whom I consider my brother, this is the rest of my family. Lord Theron, Astor, Prince Daire, and Prince Fallon." I wink at them all.

"They're not family. Family are those with whom you share blood," Caro states, then glances at Valerian. "Or your husband, mate, whatever."

"Unfortunately, I grew up without blood relatives, so I've

learned to find and adopt my family," I explain. "Is there a problem? Because we can leave." I keep my face impassive. The thought of leaving without answers would be a blow, but I won't deny my family.

Solandis gives Caro her best haughty stare and a warning. "I consider Arden my family, my daughter, blood or not. I recommend you weigh your actions carefully. Offending the light Fae, especially the sister of the queen, is not something to undertake lightly. At the very least, we would need to involve the Supernatural Council."

Nico Perrone whispers something in Caro's ear. She exhales loudly. "Fine. They can stay. Let's get started." With a glare towards my entourage, she waves a hand at someone in the crowd.

I exhale slowly in relief, and Valerian squeezes my hand.

Bianca comes forward. "Hello, Arden, dear. I'll be conducting your final two tests." She motions me to the center of the room, where a simple wooden chair sits.

"Do we have any volunteers?" she calls out to the crowd.

Santiago steps forward. "I'll volunteer." He sits down in the chair.

Bianca conjures a knife, then looks to me. "Are you ready?"

I nod.

She slices Santiago's arm from elbow to wrist. He winces and turns to me.

Thinking about Daire's instructions, I think about the fact that he's Reyna's sole parent, her father, whom she cares for very much. He helped me learn how to transfigure, and he stayed at Amelie's side when she confessed her mixed heritage.

My hands begin to glow, and I place them over him. The crowd murmurs behind me, but I ignore them. Finally, I bring up the memory of him fighting beside me when the assassins attacked. His skin knits together, and I pull my hands away.

"He's healed," Bianca calls out. "Arden is confirmed to have an affinity for five bloodlines." She motions for Santiago to return to the crowd. "Now, we'll test for bloodline six. Arden, whenever you're ready, you'll need to transform into another creature to prove your affinity to the bloodline." She moves to the edge of the circle.

I stare at my family, whose faces display zero emotion, but their gazes are intent.

Cassandra, Caro, and Clare look smug standing on the side of the circle. The crowd is quiet, almost holding their breath in anticipation.

Building the picture in my head, I spool spirit from its source and wrap it around the image in my head. Stroking it softly, I will it to life. The intense heat sweeps over me, changing me molecule by molecule, until I'm standing in the same spot, but on foreign legs.

"This is a lie!" shouts Caro. She stands in front of me. "What magic did you use to conjure this…this…dragon?" She marches over to Valerian and sneers. "Did you change her?"

He roars at Caro. "Are you accusing me of tampering with your ceremony? Think carefully, witch. The dragons have not gone to war in a long time, but that can change." He crosses his arms. "I didn't change Arden into a dragon. It's not possible." He snarls down at Caro. Glancing at me, he continues, "Lass, you're a beautiful dragon." His eyes shine with emotion as he stares at me.

In my mind, I change the picture to the unicorn from the other day, then transform again. The crowd shuffles, pointing at me, which makes Caro turn back around. I shake my mane and neigh at her.

"Santiago! Where are you? Step forward," she commands loudly.

Santiago steps forward. "Yes, Caro?" He raises an eyebrow, clearly irritated with her lack of respect.

"How can Arden have an affinity for bloodline six?" she

asks him.

"Apparently, one of my ancestors had a secret affair," he replies baldly. "Wily old goat, always flaunting the rules. A few hundred years ago, a Martinez had an affair with a Franca Perrone. It resulted in a child, Gia Perrone." He turns to address the crowd. "If Arden can trace her lineage back to Gia Perrone, then she can claim an affinity to bloodline six." His eyes cut over to mine, a question in their depths.

Picturing myself in the amber dress, I transform back. Exhaustion rolls over me, and I sway from the effort it took to complete two transformations. "I am a descendant of Gia Perrone." My voice rings out in confirmation. The noise from the crowd increases as everyone talks. I look over to Solandis and see a glimpse of sadness in her eyes at the mention of my mother.

Bianca steps forward. "Arden has an affinity to all six bloodlines. The testing concludes, and the results are final." Bianca makes a mark on the tablet and steps closer to me.

"Welcome to the family," she whispers. "Brace yourself." Handing the tablet to Caro, she walks over to stand close to my family, quietly declaring her allegiance.

Caro hisses at her in anger, while the furious expression on Nico Perrone's face is the first sign that all hell is about to break loose.

Without giving him a chance to speak, I blurt out, "I've tested for all the bloodlines, isn't it time for the placement ceremony?" I hold my breath while I wait for Caro to get a grip on her anger and resume the ceremony. If my theory is correct, this is the part she needs the most.

Clare grips her arm, urging her to focus. "You're quite right. It's time for the ceremony. The bowl will test your blood, and if worthy, the rowan will capture your name on the tree. Follow me." Her heels click hard on the marble floor as she walks over to the bowl. It's sitting on a table in front of the tapestry.

She motions for me to step up to the table. "As you can see, the bowl has a thorn on it. Place your palm down sharply on the bowl and let your blood flow into it. Your blood will mingle with that of all the witches across time, telling us of your place within our coven. If accepted into the coven, the tapestry weaves your name into the appropriate family branch." Her eyes cut to Nico Perrone for a brief second.

Taking a deep breath, I glance at Astor, who nods subtly. Without further thought, I slam my hand down on the thorn. The bowl seals to my hand, cementing it to the thorn, while my blood drips down to pool in the bottom. It swirls, mingling with the blood from past witches, until they become one.

The crowd moans, and Caro cackles. "Your blood is very powerful, more than I even guessed," she moans ecstatically, clutching Nico's shoulder, while my power courses through her and every other witch in the room.

It's just as I thought. The bowl binds the blood of the witches. Every drop of my blood binds us closer and closer together. I can feel the thoughts and power of every witch here. While several witches, like Caro, Cassandra, Santiago, and a few others, burn bright with power, the rest are muffled, their power a splinter of mine.

Caro turns and gapes at the tapestry. A golden light appears, her fists clench, and she looks at me in disbelief. "It appears you've been accepted into the coven. Congratulations," she spits out, her jaw locked tightly in anger.

The golden light whizzes across the family names, flitting between Perrone and the edge of the tapestry, until suddenly, dust flies from the edge when it picks the corner to weave my name.

Everyone stops and stares at it, unclear as to what they're witnessing.

When the last letter of my name is woven into the tapestry, the razor thin layer over the tapestry dissolves, leaving a different, older version of the tree. Witches scramble to get closer to the tapestry to study the changes, and I subtly remove my hand from the bowl.

The family branches displayed on the tapestry have increased from six to seven, the seventh branch appearing directly in the middle, a part of the trunk tapering into a thick branch. The name MacAllister is displayed on the seventh branch for everyone to see.

Above each of the seven branches, seven races are listed. Amelie steps forward, her eyes wide with horror. Fae is written above bloodline two, her bloodline, and bloodline five, the elemental bloodline. I glance at Theron, but he's also staring at the tapestry.

Demon is above bloodline three, Elven is listed above bloodlines one and four, shifter is listed above bloodline six, and dragon above bloodline seven. I glance at Santiago, whose look of satisfaction tells me he already knew they were descended from shifters, just like Amelie knew about her Fae ancestry.

Shouting amongst the witches in the crowd tell me they were clueless about their hybrid ancestry, and that dragons were the source of the MacAllister ancestry. I glance over at Valerian.

Valerian's face is a picture of horror, while his eyes move rapidly from leaf to leaf.

Puzzled, I turn back to the tree to read the names of the MacAllisters, along with the dates of their births and deaths. An unexpected pattern emerges. Over half of the leaves have the same date of death. Hundreds of MacAllisters died the same day as Moira and her family.

Stunned, I double-check every leaf. While I know Valerian's father and his dragons wiped out Moira and her family, they didn't wipe out the entire clan. But someone or something tried. On the same day. One small MacAllister branch remains on the tapestry, a few leaves on it. Both Caro and I step closer to those leaves. The names are burned off, only holes in their place.

I back away until I can see the entire tapestry again. My eyes scan for answers.

Drawn back to the corner where my name is embroidered in glowing gold threads, I see the words "The Rowan" above my name. And pinned to the tapestry, a sheaf of papers waits for someone to pick them up.

Caro reaches to grab them, but she can't. No matter how hard she tries, she can't pick them up. She gestures for Nico and Cassandra to try, but the papers refuse to budge.

The papers flutter in my direction, waving softly at me. I walk over and pull them carefully away from the tapestry. The paper is thick and stiff and old, thousands of years old if I were to guess, and they're addressed to the Rowan. Am I the Rowan?

Caro strides over to me and demands, "You'll give me those papers. I'm the leader of the coven, and since you're now a member, you answer to me." She swipes a hand at the papers, but I pull them out of her reach.

"Let's get a few things straight, shall we?" I tuck the papers under my arm, then continue, "As one of the oldest and most powerful witches here, I believe your leadership of the coven is in question."

"Oldest?" she scoffs, amused by my words.

"Gia Perrone was my mother. She gave the Princess of the Light Fae guardianship of me when I was a baby, three hundred and twenty-eight years ago. I believe that makes me one of the oldest in this room. Not the oldest, you understand," I explain, pointing to Daire and Astor. "Those two are much older than me."

"If you're that old, you're immortal and not a pure witch," she states gleefully. "Only pure witches can be a part of the coven. Witches with mixed heritage aren't allowed, because their very existence weakens us, diluting our witch powers."

It's my turn to be smug. "According to that tapestry, neither are you. Every witch family is descended from another race. It's the source of our magic. But for some reason, they've hidden this heritage from us for a long time." I scrutinize the crowd. "Your exclusiveness is making you weaker, not stronger. I'm the perfect example. I'm powerful, with an affinity to all six blood-lines, and I'm mixed blood. I know every single witch felt my power when the thorn drank my blood. Did my powers feel diluted? Of course not. My immortality gives me the stamina to use my powers. It doesn't detract from them. The reason you're weak is because you haven't infused new blood into your line in over a thousand years." I wave at the tapestry. "It's right there for you to read. Open your eyes. If you don't mate with other races, your children and your children's children will be so weak, their power will fall to human levels."

The crowd gasps, and arguments break out as individuals take sides. Realizing the crowd is distracted, I glance at Astor. With a flash, he burns every drop of my blood.

As my blood burns in the bowl, my wrist burns, too. I look down in disbelief when the words "The Rowan" and a tree show up, tattooed onto my wrist. Lifting it up, I subtly show it to Theron. He frowns, studying it for a second, before blowing an icy wind to soothe the sting. He tucks my hand into the crook of his arm to hide the tattoo.

Suddenly glad that Caro invited the entire coven to my cere-mony, I murmur to Theron I'm ready to leave. He signals to Valerian, who steps up on my left. Flanked by them both, I stuff the papers in my clutch and walk over to Caro.

"I can see you're busy, so we'll let ourselves out," I announce. The crowd around her quiets. "But don't worry, I'll be in touch. If the witches are to recover our future, we need changes, starting at the top."

She steps up to my face. "Over my dead body," she spits out. "I've given everything to this coven. It's mine."

"I wouldn't say that too loudly," I reply, eyeing the angry red faces around her. "Have a good evening."

35

ARDEN

E merging from the portal, I stand staring at The Abbey in front of me. Instead of dark and forbidding, the sight of the dark grey brick evokes a feeling of warmth and safety, like home. Valerian touches my arm in inquiry, and I shake my head.

"It's nothing. Just happy to be home," I reassure him.

At the word home, he beams, then wraps his arms around me. "Home," he repeats. "I like the sound of that word on your lips."

Astor holds the door open. "Hurry," he shouts. "I'm dying to know what's in those papers."

With a roll of my eyes, I slip out of Valerian's arms and stroll through the door, where I find everyone waiting for me.

"Let's head up to the VIP area. I could use a drink," I say, heading to the staircase. Between the healing, transforming twice, and losing all that blood, I'm swaying lightly with exhaustion. Daire swings me into his arms and carries me up the stairs.

"Thank you," I murmur.

After putting me down, he snags a bottle of Macallan and a few glasses. Pouring a healthy amount into each, he hands me one and takes one for himself. As the others arrive, everyone grabs a glass of whisky except for Solandis, who conjures up a glass of her favorite wine.

After taking a few sips, I pull the papers from my clutch and lay them on the table. There are three pieces of paper, but one feels newer than the others, so I start with that one.

I pull it from the pile, and stare at it. "It's a letter..." I glance over to Solandis and continue, "from my mother."

She inches forward on the sofa and clasps my hand tightly. "She didn't say anything," she says. "If you want to read it privately, we'll understand."

My thoughts race while I stare down at the letter. No more secrets. I straighten it out and start reading it aloud.

My darling Arden,

If you're reading this letter, you've reached the first and most important step on the path to your destiny. You are the Rowan. I know you don't understand what that means, yet. Unfortunately, it's going to take time to unravel your future, but I'll do my best to guide you without interfering in your destiny.

Gemma Perrone, our ancestor, lived during the time of the MacAllister massacre. She saw a disturbing future for all witches and decided to intervene, hoping she could change it. Her visions guided her to save a young MacAllister witch, the key to saving the seventh bloodline and the future of witches everywhere.

She convinced the witch to leave her family and travel far away, to hide herself and her bloodline from everyone around her. Through her, the MacAllister line would survive, and one day, from her line, would come the Rowan.

The MacAllister clan used to be the strongest witch family, the branch that grew from the trunk, and they believed their strength came from the mating of a witch and another non-human race. They often found their mate within the dragon clans. When the dragons turned on them, the other six families jumped at an opportunity to destroy the MacAllisters once and for all, setting the witches on the path to purifying their blood.

You, the Rowan, are the only witch from all seven bloodlines. With your blood, the keys to the past are unlocked, the tapestry and our original heritage revealed to all. If the witches are to survive, they must embrace their origins and seek other races to strengthen their family lines again. With you leading them, they will survive better than ever.

I bound your powers when you were younger to prevent your father's family from finding you. Now that you've found your witch heritage, the binding is broken. Search for the MacAllister matriarch's journals, and they will lead you to your other half, the home of your father. Once you are whole, your ultimate destiny will become clear.

Tell Solandis she did a remarkable job raising you and I miss her terribly. And when you see your father, tell him I don't regret a thing. When you find your lovers and mates, you'll know how I feel.

I love you, my darling.
Your mother, Gia Perrone

STUNNED, I SIT THERE STARING AT THE LETTER. I HEAR A delicate sniffle and turn to Solandis. "She's right. I couldn't have asked for better parents than you two," I whisper, not trusting my voice. "Without you both, I wouldn't be the person I am today. I love you." I reach over and pull Solandis into my arms for a hug, then Vargas.

My eyes find Valerian's, and I ache for the anger and utter wretchedness I see in his eyes. "We'll make this right," I vow. We will find a way to honor the MacAllisters.

He gives me a determined nod.

I sit back and pick up the second paper. There's a verse written on it.

THE ROWAN, HIDDEN AND FREE,
Dark and light battle for thee,
Nature gives life and purpose,
Nurture gives power and drive,
When the one binds the five.
Only then can the Prime decide.

"I HATE PROPHECIES AND OBSCURE LINES OF FATE," I GROWL, brave and calm on the outside, but inside, I'm anxious. Am I strong enough? Smart enough? What if I fail? Is the world going to end?

But a kernel of excitement worms its way into my thoughts. Can I find my father? Is he still alive, or am I hunting for a ghost? He's immortal, but anything could have happened in the last three hundred and twenty-eight years. I remind myself that my mother was a seer and would have foreseen his death. But then again, I wonder why she didn't foresee her own. Or maybe she did.

Sighing, I pick up the last paper. It's blank. I hand it to Theron, who studies it, then passes it around to the others. They all look puzzled, then Astor tries a reveal spell, but nothing happens.

When it comes back to me, I stare down at it. "Now what?"

I almost drop it when script appears on the paper.

Find the journals.

THANK YOU!

Thank you! I hope you enjoyed this new world of mine, and will consider writing a review for this book. As a new author, writing is both scary and wonderful. Creating characters and worlds in your head, trying to get them cohesively on paper, then putting them out there for the world to view is daunting. Whether it's "give me more" or "I think this character needs more love", reviews help me write the next story.

*If you find an error, please feel free to email me at Stellabrie@stellabrie.com.

ACKNOWLEDGMENTS

Huge thanks to everyone who made this book possible! Both, my husband and mom, who put up with my incessant plot and character discussions.

My beta readers, who caught so many big and little things! I know this book is better because of you. Thank you - Nia, Bianca, Sherri Ann, Melissa, Amber, and of course, my mom, for all of your feedback!

My gorgeous cover is by Mayflower Studio. Amala does fabulous work! Check her out.

Rockstar editing and proofreading by two lovely ladies, Meghan at Bookish Dreams Editing and Nicole at Proof Before You Publish.

ABOUT THE AUTHOR

Stella Brie lives outside of Nashville, TN, with her husband and golden retriever, Bailey. After mentioning her desire to write a book a million times to her husband, he challenged her to sit down one day and write a paragraph. Instead, she wrote her first book, My Salvation, and achieved her dream.

She decided to trade in her career in digital marketing, working on big brands, for this wildly creative one. Armed with a notebook, crammed full of ideas, she is constantly thinking about bold heroines, sexy men, and HEAs. Whether it's a paranormal book full of creatures and magic or a contemporary romance full of heat and drama, she's always thinking about how she can bring her books to life.

Latest News and Updates:
    Facebook Group: Stella's Stalkers
    Instagram: @stellabrie_author
    Twitter: @stella_brie
    Website / Newsletter: Official Stella Brie

    facebook.com/AuthorStellaBrie
    instagram.com/stellabrie_author
    amazon.com/author/stellabrie

ALSO BY STELLA BRIE

My Salvation - Contemporary Reverse Harem

When an act of violence shatters her life and dreams, Dr. Kate Michaels is forced into a nomadic existence.

Another town, another assignment. Content to live life one day at a time, Kate self-isolates to protect herself from the fear and judgment of others. In Montana for her latest job, will she find love and salvation with four scintillating men, or will she let the past hold her back?

Brothers by choice, they lost hope when the woman they loved left them. Can they open their battered hearts and trust again?

Sexy Lev, full of laughter and sunshine, with so much love to give.

Icy, controlled Lowell…is there more behind the façade?

Shaw, fierce and commanding, protecting his family against further heartache.

Lost and hurting, can Thayer let go of his destructive ways and embrace his future?